This book belongs to

_____

*Hidden in the broom cupboard
of Rose Cottage are two grand gates
that lead to the loveliest little house
you've ever seen. Nutmouse Hall.
Shh, don't tell anyone . . . No one
knows it's there . . . not even
Arthur and Lucy who live
in Rose Cottage.*

*This is the home of
Tumtum and Nutmeg . . .*

EGMONT

We bring stories to life

First published 2008
by Egmont UK Limited
239 Kensington High Street, London W8 6SA

ISBN 978 1 4052 3386 6

3 5 7 9 10 8 6 4 2

www.egmont.co.uk

A CIP catalogue record for this title is available
from the British Library

Typeset by Avon DataSet Ltd, Bidford on Avon, Warwickshire
Printed and bound in Italy by L.E.G.O. S.P.A

TUMTUM and NUTMEG

by Emily Bearn

Illustrated by Nick Price

EGMONT

For Freya

Chapter One

Once there were two married mice called Mr and Mrs Nutmouse, and they lived in great style. They had a big, rambling house with a ballroom, and a billiards room, and a banqueting room, and a butler's room, and just about every other sort of room a married couple might want. (There were thirty-six rooms in all.)

The house was called Nutmouse Hall, and it

was situated in the broom cupboard of a small human dwelling called Rose Cottage. A broom cupboard might not sound a very grand place for a house, but this broom cupboard was special. It had creamy white walls, and mottled red tiles on the floor, and a tiny sash window hidden behind a curtain of honeysuckle.

But the nicest thing of all about the broom cupboard was that no human knew it was there. This is because, a very long time ago, soon after Rose Cottage was built, someone pushed a big Welsh dresser against the kitchen wall, hiding the broom cupboard door from view; and the dresser always stayed there, because there was nowhere else to put it.

It was Mr Nutmouse's great-great-great-grandfather who first discovered the broom cupboard, when he crept beneath the dresser, and poked his nose under the door. The red tiles and the white walls looked so appealing that he decided to build a house there straight away; and the first thing he had to do was to build a big round mouse-hole so that his workmen could get in and out with all their bricks and cement-mixers. Then he fitted the mouse-hole with smart iron gates, and as soon as a mouse entered those gates he was on the Nutmouse family's territory.

Nutmouse Hall was built in the middle of the broom cupboard, and it was considered a very fine piece of architecture. The walls were made of pretty pebblestone, and there were gables on the windows and little turrets peeking out of the roof. The front of the house faced south, so the bedroom windows caught the sun as it filtered through the honey-suckle. The smallest rooms, such as the bathrooms, were the size of a cake-tin, while the ballroom was the size of a hamper. (And a hamper-sized room seemed very big to the Nutmouses, since they were only two inches long.)

Because Nutmouse Hall was so enormous, Mr and Mrs Nutmouse did not use all the rooms available to them. Mr Nutmouse spent most of the time in his library, warming his toes in front of the fire, and Mrs Nutmouse spent most of her time scurrying about in her kitchen, making delicious things to eat.

Mr and Mrs Nutmouse had been married a long time, but they still called each other by the affectionate pet names they had adopted during their engagement. Mrs Nutmouse called Mr Nutmouse Tumtum, because he had such a large one, and Mr Nutmouse called Mrs Nutmouse Nutmeg, because she had nutmeg hair. (Mr Nutmouse thought this was very exotic, because his family had all been greys.)

In their funny way, the Nutmouses were well-suited to each other. Mr Nutmouse was a wise, bookish sort of mouse. He never lost his temper or got agitated, and he did everything very calmly and slowly. Mrs Nutmouse was quite the opposite. She did everything very fast, and even little tasks, such as putting the icing on a cake, could get her into a terrible dither. But in her hasty way she was surprisingly efficient. The house was spick and span, the bills were paid on time, and the food served at Nutmouse Hall was the envy of all the mice for miles around.

Mrs Nutmouse looked upon every meal as a celebration. For breakfast there would be eggs and bacon and toast and marmalade; lunch was all manner of cold meats and salads; for tea there was always a homemade cake or scone; and supper would be a delicacy, such as earwigs *en croute*. Mrs Nutmouse had a whole shelf of cookery books, so she was never short of inspiration.

Mr Nutmouse was not as rich as his ancestors had been, and this was because he gave most of his money away. He supported all sorts of charities — charities for homeless mice, charities for arthritic mice, charities for illiterate mice, charities for bald

mice . . . he even supported a charity for mice with hiccups. So one way or another the Nutmouses did not have much money left. They did not employ a butler or a maid; and they could not afford to give banquets in their banqueting room, nor balls in their ballroom.

But since neither of them much liked balls and banquets, they didn't mind a bit; and Mrs Nutmouse was such a good housekeeper that life was splendid all the same.

But beyond the broom cupboard, where the humans lived, things were not splendid at all. Rose Cottage was owned by Mr Mildew, a widower who lived there with his two children, Arthur and Lucy. They were very poor, and they did not have nearly so many rooms as the Nutmouses had. There was one bathroom, which was only a little bit bigger than the bath, and Arthur and Lucy shared a tiny bedroom in the attic with a ceiling that leaked.

From the outside, Rose Cottage looked very inviting. The garden was full of pear trees and wild flowers, and the honeysuckle trailed all over the stone walls, and curled along the fat fringe of the thatch. But inside it was less agreeable. Every room was rife with clutter and chaos, the walls were damp, and the plaster was beginning to crumble. The beams in the sitting room were full of woodworm, and the carpets were so threadbare you could see through to the floorboards, which were full of woodworm too. The boiler had packed up long ago, and in winter the wind howled into the kitchen through the cracks in the garden door.

The cottage had been much better cared for when Mrs Mildew was alive, but she had died long ago, when Arthur was still a baby. He couldn't remember his mother at all, and Lucy could only remember her lying in bed looking very thin and white, with a fat doctor standing over her. Lucy had been told the name of her mother's illness once, but it had been much too peculiar a word for her to remember.

The Mildew children did not miss having a mother, because they couldn't remember what having one had been like. And yet they knew that there were certain disadvantages to being without one, and they considered living in chaos to be among them.

But Mr Mildew was such a head-in-the-clouds sort of fellow that he hardly seemed to notice how squalid Rose Cottage had become. He was an inventor by trade, and he spent all his time crashing about in his tiny study upstairs, trying to invent things. Years ago, he had invented a gadget for peeling grapes, which had been sold in a department store in London and had made him quite rich for a short time. But people weren't buying his grape-peelers any more, so now he needed to invent something else.

And as a result, he didn't think nearly as hard as he might about the housekeeping, which was why Rose Cottage was such a mess. It was all he could do to put meals on the table, and he was so absent-minded that he could never remember which meal was which. So as often as not Arthur and Lucy found themselves eating tinned spaghetti for breakfast, and porridge for supper.

The Mildews all looked rather scruffy, for they never had haircuts or new clothes, but there was something distinguished about them too. Lucy was tall and graceful, and she had hair the colour of copper; and Arthur had blue eyes and thick black curls, and he wore glasses with a broken frame which kept slipping off his nose. Mr Mildew was the most striking of all – he always dressed in a purple smoking jacket, which was falling to bits, and he had wiry hair which stuck out of his head like insect antennae.

Less imaginative children might have been embarrassed by Mr Mildew, but Arthur and Lucy felt

proud of him because he was much more interesting and exotic than anyone else's father. And he had plenty of good points. He hardly ever lost his temper, and he never nagged them to do boring things, like cleaning their teeth, or brushing their hair, or tidying their room, or doing their homework. But it wasn't easy living with someone quite so absent-minded, and now and again they did feel a bit neglected.

And at the time this story begins they had reason to feel even more neglected than usual. It was the middle of a long, icy winter – they had known weeks and weeks of the sort of biting weather that makes it painful to be outdoors. No one could remember the village being as cold. The duck pond was frozen to its depths, the gargoyles on the church were dribbling icicles, and all the school water pipes had frozen solid. One night, two of them burst.

This was a great drama, and it meant that the school had to be closed for seven whole weeks while something called 'essential renovations' took place. Most of the children were very pleased about this, for it's not every year that one's Christmas holiday is extended until February. But Arthur and Lucy weren't so pleased. For if you have a father who gives you tinned spaghetti for breakfast, and a cottage so cold that the butter freezes in the kitchen, then the prospect of being stuck at home all winter long is not especially appealing.

Had they known that there were mice living such gracious lives in their broom cupboard, they might have felt quite envious. They might even have wished they were mice themselves, so that they could move into Nutmouse Hall and live as the Nutmouses did.

And had the Nutmouses been different, they might have sniffed down their noses at the Mildews, and felt quite superior and cock-a-hoop. But Mr and Mrs Nutmouse did not feel cock-a-hoop at all. As a matter of fact, they felt rather uncomfortable. They were kind-hearted mice, and they did not think it right that they should be eating sumptuous meals in a warm house, while the Mildew children ate horrid things like tinned spaghetti in their icy kitchen.

The Nutmouses had been concerned about Arthur and Lucy for some time, and the colder the winter became, the more their concern grew. And there comes a point at which a concern grows so big that something has to be done about it.

Chapter Two

A few days after the school pipes burst, it started to snow. It was only fleeting at first, and when the Nutmouses poked their noses outdoors after breakfast it looked as if it might not settle. But it snowed all day, thicker and faster, and by tea time the whole village had been blanketed.

Shortly after four o'clock, Mrs Nutmouse visited the Mildews' kitchen to borrow a few bits and pieces for her bread and butter pudding. There was snow blustering in under the garden door and it was so cold that she could see her breath making little grey clouds in the air.

She didn't linger long, for the Mildews seldom had much worth borrowing, and this afternoon there was even less than usual. There were neither currants nor cinnamon in the cupboard, and nothing on the floor but a bit of squished banana. There was a scrap of fruit cake left on the table, but it was so stale that when Mrs Nutmouse bumped into it she stubbed her toe. And when she climbed on to the toast rack to poke her nose down inside the milk bottle, she could see a film of white ice. Brrrrr! Drawing her woollen cape tight round her shoulders, she chiselled a corner off a pat of frosty butter, then she scuttled as fast as she could back to Nutmouse Hall.

Mr Nutmouse was in the kitchen, leaning against the stove. He was hoping for his tea.

'Oh, Tumtum, I don't know what's to become of those Mildews,' Mrs Nutmouse said forlornly, plonking her wicker basket on the table. 'Their kitchen's so cold that the milk's started to freeze, and all the cupboards are bare. They need a fairy godmother to take charge of them.'

Mrs Nutmouse longed to go through Rose Cottage with her mop and pail, scrubbing and darning and mending and mothering, and fuss-potting about from top to bottom; but she was only a mouse, so what use could she possibly be? She couldn't even lift one of the Mildews' saucers!

Mr Nutmouse looked thoughtful. He knew

that Mrs Nutmouse was upset about the conditions next door, and he had something to propose.

'How about a little tea, Nutmeg dear?' he said, for he never liked proposing things on an empty stomach.

Mrs Nutmouse scurried about the kitchen, and laid the table with a dainty blue and white teapot, and homemade gingerbread, and macaroons, and cucumber sandwiches, and scones with butter and damson jam; but she was feeling too upset to eat more than a few crumbs.

'Oh, if only we could help them, Tumtum!' she sighed, watching him tuck in.

'Perhaps we can,' he replied mysteriously. Then he retrieved a crumpled piece of paper from his waistcoat pocket, and studied it through his spectacles.

'I had a look around the attic this morning, while the children were asleep, and I made a list of one or two things we could do,' he said. 'For a start, I could repair the electric heater –'

'*Repair the heater?*' Mrs Nutmouse asked incredulously. 'How do you intend to do that?'

'Very simply,' Mr Nutmouse replied, helping himself to a fat slice of gingerbread. 'I just need to crawl inside and do a spot of rewiring – it's the sort of thing a mouse can do much more easily than a human.' Mr Nutmouse was keen on rewiring – he'd once rewired the whole of Nutmouse Hall.

Mrs Nutmouse beamed. 'What a good idea, Tumtum!' she said. 'Then the children won't have to sleep in their duffel coats any more.'

'Quite so,' Mr Nutmouse said, feeling rather pleased with himself. 'And there's plenty more we can see to. Arthur's glasses are about to fall apart, because there are two screws loose in the frame. So I'll take my drill up to the attic, and tighten them again.'

'Tumtum, how wonderful!' Mrs Nutmouse cried. 'And what can I do?'

'All sorts of things,' he said reassuringly. 'You can darn some of their clothes, for a start. You're a fast sewer, and if you do a small amount each evening, everything will be mended within a week or so. And you can patch their shoes too, using the leather from that old armchair in my dressing room – I've never much liked it anyway, it's rather in the way there. And why not use your washing line to replace the lace in Arthur's boot? You hardly need it any more, now that we've got a tumble-dryer . . .'

And so Mr Nutmouse went on, suggesting more and more ingenious ways to help.

'When can we start?' Mrs Nutmouse asked eagerly, feeling much too excited to drink her tea.

'There's no time like the present,' Mr Nutmouse said. 'I vote we set out tonight.'

Mrs Nutmouse agreed, and that was how the adventures began.

Shortly after ten o'clock, Mrs Nutmouse pressed her little brown nose through the front gate, and twitched it back and forth under the dresser. Twitch! Twitch! Twitch!

'All clear, Tumtum!' she called back to her

husband, who was following behind her carrying a wooden toolbox and a drill, and dragging the bulky leather chair cover. Mrs Nutmouse was carrying her sewing basket and her mop and pail, and also the washing line which was wound round her shoulder like a lasso.

They crossed the kitchen floor and crept into the hall, then they dragged all their clobber up the skirting board which ran along the stairs, and tiptoed across the landing. There was light glinting beneath the study door, and when they peeked underneath it they could see Mr Mildew crouched on the floor, amid a sea of brightly coloured wires and tiny shards of metal. His face was purple, and he was cursing under his breath: 'Damned creature!'

'I wonder what he's inventing now,' Mrs Nutmouse whispered.

'A battery-operated mouse that gobbles all the crumbs off a dinner table, like a Hoover,' Mr Nutmouse said knowingly. 'I heard him telling Arthur about it. He thinks it's going to make him rich again. It's called The Hungry House Mouse.'

'Goodness,' Mrs Nutmouse said. 'What a curious idea! I wonder why it's making him so cross.'

'I believe he's got the mechanics wrong,' Mr Nutmouse said. 'Instead of a hungry mouse, he's invented an unusually delicate one. No sooner has it gobbled the crumbs, than it sicks them all up again.'

'What a waste!' Mrs Nutmouse said, shaking her head disapprovingly. 'A real mouse would do the job much better.'

The mice pressed on, and heaved their things up the steep stairs to the attic. The room was bitterly cold, for there were no curtains to keep out the draught, and they had to blow on their paws to stop them from going numb. They had trouble getting their bearings for it was quite dark at first, but then the clouds scudded in the wind and the moon shone through the window on to the children's beds. Arthur was completely buried under his blankets, but they could see Lucy's hair on her pillow shining red in the moonlight.

The mice worked furiously. Mr Nutmouse got the heater going and drilled Arthur's glasses back into shape, and Mrs Nutmouse darned three pairs of socks and swept out both the children's satchels; then she climbed into the basin with her

mop and polished it until it became so slippery she couldn't stand up again. Mr Nutmouse had to throw the plug down to her so she could clamber free up the chain.

Finally she scuttled off into the wardrobe to start mending Arthur and Lucy's clothes. They were so full of holes that Mrs Nutmouse reckoned it would take her weeks to get through them all, and some were so threadbare it was hardly worth mending them at all. As she persevered with her tiny needle, she could hear the children's soft, steady breathing from the other side of the room; they were deeply asleep, quite innocent of all the bustle that was going on.

Mrs Nutmouse felt very protective of them. *Mr Mildew is simply not capable of looking after two children on his own*, she thought sternly, setting to work on a gaping hole in the elbow of one of Arthur's jerseys. *They need a mother, and in the absence of a human one, I will have to do.* And as she set herself the responsibility of mothering the Mildews, Mrs Nutmouse felt a warm glow in her stomach. She and Tumtum had never had a litter of their own, and she considered herself blessed to be able to adopt two human children instead.

The mice beavered away until midnight, when they decided to stop for a rest. Mrs Nutmouse had tucked two slices of fruit cake and a thermos of tea into her sewing basket, and they both felt much in need of them.

'Bother!' she said, unpacking the picnic. 'I forgot to pack any plastic cups.'

'Never mind,' said Mr Nutmouse, who could feel his tummy rumbling. 'We can swig from the thermos.'

But Mrs Nutmouse was more particular about such things. 'Look, Tumtum!' she cried, pointing towards a tall pink building in the corner. 'Lucy's doll's house! It's sure to have a tea service!'

The mice walked towards it, and peered through the drawing room window. It was not nearly so big as their drawing room at Nutmouse Hall, but it was prettily furnished, with pale blue curtains and a grand piano. There were two dolls made of pipe-cleaners sitting on the sofa, and there was a case full of books by the fire. Something about the house seemed to beckon them inside.

They passed underneath the white awning,

and pushed on the front door. It swung open, leading into an airy hall with a coat stand, and a grandfather clock. To the right was the kitchen, in which there stood a trestle table, with benches down each side. There were lots of pots and pans hanging above the stove, and Mrs Nutmouse found a whole hotchpotch of mismatched china in one of the cupboards. Everything was mouse-sized.

Mrs Nutmouse laid the table, and they both sat down feeling very civilised.

'We've still got an awful lot to do,' Mrs Nutmouse said wearily. 'And if we don't finish tonight, we'll have to lug all our stuff back upstairs again tomorrow night.'

'We needn't do that, Nutmeg,' Mr Nutmouse replied. 'We could leave everything here, in the doll's house. We can tuck it all away somewhere, so Lucy won't find it.'

'Oh, Tumtum, what a good idea!' she cried. 'Then we can just come back and do more chores whenever we've time.'

So they worked for another hour or so, then they crept back to the doll's house and put the toolbox and the sewing basket in the cupboard under the stairs. The mop and pail wouldn't fit, so Mrs Nutmouse hid them behind the kitchen door.

Then, by instinct, she cleared away their cups and plates from the table and put them in the doll's house sink. There was no running water, but she could fill it next time with her bucket. 'I do so like this doll's house, Tumtum. It feels a bit like camping,' Mrs Nutmouse said, and she thought that next time she came she would bring a new tablecloth for the kitchen.

Mr Nutmouse was longing to get home, for he was quite exhausted, but Mrs Nutmouse found it a wrench to leave. She would have given anything to have seen the children's faces when they woke up to find their heater working, for by now the attic was lovely and warm.

'We could spend the night here,' she suggested, but Mr Nutmouse was having none of it.

'That would be very rash, Nutmeg,' he said. 'They might see us!' They both agreed that would not do at all, for some humans have funny feelings towards mice; so Mr Nutmouse took his wife by the paw, and they scuttled back to Nutmouse Hall and collapsed into their four-poster bed.

Chapter Three

Mr and Mrs Nutmouse became regular visitors to the attic, and thought of more and more things to do. Mr Nutmouse bought a bag of cement, and used it to seal all the little cracks in the attic windowpanes. And he climbed up into the roof, and patched the leak with a big roll of linoleum which he'd stripped out of one of the bathrooms in Nutmouse Hall. Mrs Nutmouse polished Arthur's train set, and mopped the children's shoes, and she spent one entire night sorting out their sock drawer. She also left tiny presents under their pillows – silver candlesticks from her banqueting hall, and bars of chocolate the size of raisins.

Day after day, the children woke up to discover some new delight. Lucy was most pleased about the tidying and the mending, and Arthur was most pleased about the presents – but they were both equally mystified.

Lucy, who was the eldest, said there must be a fairy in the house. But Arthur had given up believing in fairies long ago, and he wasn't at all convinced. Then one day he opened his pencil case and found that all his pencils had been sharpened in a most peculiar way – they looked as though they'd been nibbled. *Well that can't have been done by a fairy*, he thought. *A fairy would have small, delicate teeth, not sharp, spiky ones.*

Later that week, another strange thing happened. On Friday afternoon, one of Arthur's teeth fell out, and before going to bed he put it on the chest of drawers, thinking he'd find somewhere to hide it away the next day. But when he woke up, the tooth had gone. In its place, there was a tin the size of a ten pence coin, and inside it a cake covered with white icing and walnuts – the tiniest cake either child had ever seen.

'Well, that means it must be a tooth fairy,' Lucy said firmly. 'Only tooth fairies take teeth away.'

'But tooth fairies leave money, not cakes,' Arthur said. (The tooth fairy had never come for him before, but it came for his friends, and he knew that they usually got at least fifty pence, and sometimes a pound.) 'And tooth fairies only come when you lose a tooth, but our fairy – or rather our,' he corrected himself, 'our . . . our whatever it is – it comes all the time.'

In truth, neither child knew what to think. If it wasn't a fairy, then it could be a ghost, but that was such a frightening option that neither of them liked to suggest it.

Eventually, Lucy proposed doing something decisive. 'I think we should write whoever it is a letter, asking them for tea,' she said.

'But what if it's a gh– well, what if it's, you know, something funny?' Arthur asked nervously. The thought of confronting their mysterious visitor

face to face made his stomach feel quite hollow.

'Well, whatever it is, it would be better to know,' Lucy said. Arthur wasn't so sure, but he didn't want Lucy thinking he was frightened, so he reluctantly agreed. Lucy went to her desk, and tore a sheet of paper out of an exercise book. Then, after some deliberation, she and Arthur composed a message:

To Whoever has been visiting us,

Thank you very much for everything you have done.

If you are a fairy, and not a ghost, then would you like to come and have tea with us here in the attic tomorrow?

Love from,

Arthur and Lucy Mildew.

P.S. Please come at four o'clock.

Lucy folded the piece of paper in half, and addressed one side to, *The Visitor, The Attic, Rose Cottage*. Then she left it propped up against the mirror on the chest of drawers. Arthur felt anxious all day – something told him that their visitor might not be at all like the fairies he'd seen pictures of in Lucy's books.

Mr and Mrs Nutmouse discovered the letter that night, and dragged it back to Nutmouse Hall. And they sat a long while in their kitchen, with it spread out in front of them all over the table, wondering what to do. Mrs Nutmouse longed to accept, but Mr Nutmouse forbade it.

'You certainly can't go, Nutmeg,' he said firmly. 'Imagine what a shock it would be for them to find that their visitor was a mouse!'

Forlornly, Mrs Nutmouse agreed. Humans could be so frosty towards mice – there was simply too much misunderstanding between the two species. And what if the children told Mr Mildew about them? There was no knowing how he'd react. He might try to evict them from their home, even though the Nutmouse family had been living in Rose Cottage much longer than the Mildews had.

But there was another reason why Mrs Nutmouse couldn't go to tea, and that was because conversation would be impossible. For mice have such tiny voices that the human ear can't pick up a word they say. Even when a mouse is shouting and bellowing at the top of his voice, a human hears only a faint squeal.

But Mr Nutmouse had an idea. 'You must certainly tell them that you're a fairy, not a ghost, for otherwise they might get frightened,' he said. 'But say that you can't accept their invitation to tea, because fairies aren't allowed to be seen by humans, and if they are seen, their magic powers stop working. I'm sure they'll understand that.'

Mrs Nutmouse agreed that this was a sensible solution, so she found a big piece of blotting paper (mouse writing paper would have been too small) and, in much larger handwriting than she normally used, she wrote the following reply:

My Dear Arthur and Lucy,

I am a fairy of sorts. But sadly I cannot accept your kind invitation to tea because my magic powers would fade if you were ever to set eyes on me.

But if there is anything more I can do for you, then just leave me another note on the chest of drawers.

Love from,

And she was about to sign herself 'Mrs Nutmouse', but she hesitated, thinking it sounded too mousy. So instead she put 'Nutmeg', which was much more the sort of name a fairy might have. Then, on Mr Nutmouse's advice, she added a postscript:

P.S. It is best not to tell anyone else about me, because that would make my magic powers fade too.

She folded the letter into an envelope, which she

addressed to *Arthur and Lucy Mildew, The Attic, Rose Cottage*. Then, before having his bath, Mr Nutmouse delivered it for her, tiptoeing back upstairs to leave it on the chest of drawers, leaning against the handle of Lucy's hairbrush.

When Lucy first picked up the brush next morning she didn't see the note, but then she noticed a tiny piece of paper fluttering to the floor. Mrs Nutmouse's writing was very wobbly (like a drunken spider, Mr Nutmouse always said), but she managed to decipher it using Arthur's magnifying glass.

'I wonder what a Fairy of Sorts looks like,' Arthur said when Lucy had read it out loud. A Fairy of Sorts didn't sound nearly as frightening as a ghost – in fact, it sounded rather nice – but even so he felt relieved he wouldn't actually have to meet Nutmeg, for he still felt a little unsure of her.

But Lucy was longing to meet her. 'I wonder where Fairies of Sorts live,' she said wonderingly, and she felt very frustrated to think she might never find out. But as she went to hide the letter in the drawer of her bedside table, where she put all her most important things, something about the doll's house caught her eye. She knelt down to look more closely.

She hadn't played with it for a whole week and now everything seemed different. The door knocker had been polished, and inside lots of things had been meddled with. The piano lid was open, and the kitchen sink was full of water. There was washing up on the draining board, and there was a tiny pair of pink slippers beside the bed upstairs.

Lucy felt a sudden thrill. 'Arthur,' she said urgently, 'Nutmeg has moved in.'

The Nutmouses hadn't really moved in, of course, because they had a very grand home of their own. But they looked on the doll's house as a bit of an adventure, and as the days passed they had become much bolder about making use of it. When they had been working especially late in the attic, they sometimes spent the night there – despite Mr Nutmouse's initial concerns. So when the children scrutinised each room in turn, they noticed all Mrs Nutmouse's efforts to make it more homely.

There were new gingham curtains in the kitchen, and new cushions on the drawing room sofa, and there were soft white towels in the bathroom. There were also hairs on the pillows in the bedroom: grey on one side of the bed, and brown on the other.

'She's got funny hair,' Lucy said. 'It looks a bit mousy.'

Arthur did not comment – he never noticed what people's hair was like. But when he saw how nice and cosy the Fairy of Sorts had made the doll's house, his fears of her at once evaporated. She seemed almost human. 'We should leave Nutmeg something to eat,' he said. 'If she can't have tea with us, then we might at least leave her tea in the doll's house.'

Lucy agreed, so after supper they waited until their father had disappeared to his study, then salvaged the last bit of shortbread from the biscuit tin, and crumbled part of it on to one of the little plates in the doll's house kitchen. Then they poured a teaspoonful of milk into one of the jugs, and laid a place at the table. They even supplied a tiny napkin, cut out of a cotton handkerchief. The Mildews never used napkins themselves, but Lucy thought Nutmeg might appreciate one.

Next morning, the shortbread and the milk had gone, and there was a letter on the table in the doll's house kitchen. Lucy picked up the magnifying glass, and read it out loud:

Dear Arthur and Lucy,

Thank you for a most magnificent feast. Your shortbread was superb, and I ate much more than I should have done. I must acquire the recipe one day. I hope you do not mind me making use of your

doll's house, but it is very convenient to have somewhere to leave my things.

 Love from,

 Nutmeg.

After that, Arthur and Lucy decided that they should leave Nutmeg something to eat every night. And they both agreed that life was much, much more interesting now that they had a Fairy of Sorts looking after them.

Chapter Four

Arthur and Lucy had been dreading their long winter holiday at home, but it was turning out to be more exciting than they could ever have imagined. Nutmeg visited almost every night, and when they woke up to find her funny little presents under their pillow it felt just like Christmas, even though Christmas had happened several weeks ago. (And they hadn't had nearly so many presents then as they were getting now.)

But just at the point at which they felt things could hardly get any nicer, something horrible happened. One morning, while the Mildews were all sitting down to a breakfast of tinned rice pudding, they heard a car stopping outside in the lane. Then there was the sound of someone cursing, followed by a sharp rap on the front door.

'I wonder who that could be,' Mr Mildew said anxiously – he always felt unsettled by visitors, even the postman. As he said it, the rapping started up again, cross and impatient.

His children followed him into the hall, and when he opened the door their hearts sank. For there was Aunt Ivy, and a taxi driver was trailing up the path behind her, carrying five suitcases.

'Your doorbell's not working, Walter,' she said sourly, pushing past Mr Mildew into the hall, and ignoring the children entirely. Then she went into the kitchen, flung her gloves down on the table, and said something disapproving about the mess.

Aunt Ivy lived a long way away, in a big city in Scotland, and yet somehow the Mildews always saw more of her than they would have liked. She had been married to Mr Mildew's brother, Hugh, who had run away to Africa several years ago and had never been heard of since. The children thought that if they had been married to Aunt Ivy, they'd have run away to Africa too, for there was something distinctly off-putting about her. She was tall and spiky looking, with long elasticey arms and dark, menacing eyes.

Since losing Hugh, she had started spending Christmas at Rose Cottage, and she ruined it every time. She always snapped and snarled, and gobbled all the chocolates, and her presents got meaner every year. Last time, she'd given Arthur a ping-pong ball, and Lucy a packet of plastic clothes pegs. She also had revolting habits, such as clipping her fingernails at the kitchen table, and stubbing out her cigarettes in the children's Wellington boots.

Mr Mildew had her to stay each year because of something called 'family duty', which makes people put up with all sorts of awkward things at Christmas time. But it wasn't Christmas now, it was January, and they were all very surprised to see her again. Arthur and Lucy stood at the kitchen door, looking at her in dismay.

'Now, do remind me, Ivy — should we have been expecting you?' Mr Mildew asked, shifting uncomfortably from one foot to the other.

Aunt Ivy looked at him contemptuously. 'Are you going senile, Walter? We arranged everything on the telephone only last week.'

Mr Mildew acknowledged this was possible, for the one thing he never forgot was his own forgetfulness. 'Yes, Ivy, of course . . . but do just remind me —'

'*Mice*, Walter,' she said, drumming her fingers irritably on the kitchen table.

At last, Mr Mildew's memory jogged into action. Ivy had seen not one but two mice in her sitting room in Scotland, and the sight had so upset her nerves that she had asked to stay at Rose

Cottage while a pest control company took up all her floorboards trying to find them. And he had said yes, just to get her off the telephone.

'Of course, of course. And, er, I've forgotten how long you might stay,' Mr Mildew said, trying to sound more casual than he felt.

'As long as it takes, Walter,' she said defiantly. 'I've told Pest Persecutors to turn my house upside down until they find those revolting little creatures. If there's one thing I loathe more than anything, it's *mice*.'

Aunt Ivy and her five suitcases took over the sitting room. The sofa was turned into a bed, and an entire shelf of the bookcase was cleared to make way for all her make-up and hair dye. Aunt Ivy took a good deal of care over her appearance. She painted her lips red and her eyelids green, and she dyed her hair jet black and parted it in a zigzag. She looked quite sinister.

And she didn't do any of the things that aunts normally do. She never knitted jerseys, or baked cakes, or listened to cheerful music on the radio. She just sat in the kitchen all day long, filing her nails, and looking grim. In order to avoid her, the children spent more and more time in the attic, and Mr Mildew spent even more time than he usually did locked away in his room.

The Nutmouses went to ground too, because the very sight of Aunt Ivy made them shudder. When she was last here, Mrs Nutmouse had seen her standing at the kitchen window sill, spearing a fly with the tip of her eye-liner, and Mr Nutmouse had seen her pouring boiling water on a beetle.

He had once heard her telling Mr Mildew how much she hated mice, and he dreaded to think what she'd do if she ever set eyes on them. So he determined to make sure she didn't. That morning, when he heard Aunt Ivy's voice ringing from the kitchen, he put a padlock round the gates of Nutmouse Hall, then he drew the bolts across the front door, and told Mrs Nutmouse that she was not to set foot in Rose Cottage except in a major emergency, such as running out of flour.

'It is simply too dangerous to venture out while that ill-tempered creature is here,' he said firmly, as they sat down to a lunch of cold tongue and potato salad, followed by sherry trifle. 'We must hibernate until she's gone.'

'But what about the children?' Mrs Nutmouse wailed. 'We can't stop visiting the attic, Tumtum! Imagine how bereft they'll feel!'

'It's not worth the risk, Nutmeg,' Mr Nutmouse said. 'There's something about that woman that makes my spine tingle.'

'Oh, I know, Tumtum, she makes mine tingle too,' Mrs Nutmouse replied. 'But we can't let her make us prisoners in our own home. So long as we wait until she's gone to bed, then it must be safe to move around. A couple of mice have never woken anybody.'

Mr Nutmouse looked thoughtful. It was true that every house mouse has the right to roam freely after dark. And they especially wanted to visit the attic that night because they had a rather wonderful present for the children – a five-pound note which they'd found shortly before Aunt Ivy arrived, half-buried in the snow bank by the lane in front of the cottage. They'd rolled it into a cylinder, then Mr Nutmouse had carried it home on his shoulder. And now it was leaning against their kitchen wall, waiting to be delivered.

'Oh, do let's take it tonight, Tumtum!' Mrs Nutmouse squealed for the dozenth time.

Mr Nutmouse finished his trifle, untucked his napkin from his collar, and sighed. 'All right, Nutmeg,' he said resignedly. 'We'll go.' But he felt very uneasy about it.

Much later, after supper, the mice tiptoed up to their front gate, and peeped out under the dresser.

The kitchen light was still on, and they could see Aunt Ivy's shadow cast across the floor. She was sitting at the table, smoking. They went back to Nutmouse Hall, waited an hour, then crept back to the gate . . . Aunt Ivy was still there. *Really*, Mrs Nutmouse thought disapprovingly, *no wonder she always looks so peaky, if she never goes to bed*.

Eventually, at a very late hour, they came to the gate to find the kitchen light turned off. They let themselves out and scuttled through to the hall, Mr Nutmouse carrying the note again on his shoulder. The sitting room light was on, and the door open, but there was no sign of Aunt Ivy.

Mr Nutmouse's ears pricked up as he heard water running upstairs. 'Come on, dear!' he said, turning to his wife. 'She's having a bath. We can sneak up now.'

They ran up the staircase skirting, and sped across the landing. They could hear Aunt Ivy splashing about in the bathroom, humming tunelessly; the noise made them both shudder. Finally they clambered up to the attic, and Mr Nutmouse climbed on to the chest of drawers, then unrolled the note and left it leaning against the mirror.

Mrs Nutmouse wanted to do some cleaning, but Mr Nutmouse wouldn't let her. He felt growing apprehension. 'Not tonight, Nutmeg,' he said. 'We must get back to Nutmouse Hall while Aunt Ivy's still wallowing.' So they ate the tea which the children had laid out for them in the doll's house, even though neither had much of an appetite, and then they made for home.

But as they were galloping across the upstairs landing, Mrs Nutmouse tripped up on her apron strings and landed on the floor, all four paws in the air. Oomph! It was very painful.

Mr Nutmouse pulled her to her feet. 'Are you all right, dear?' he asked anxiously.

'Oh, yes, yes, Tumtum! Nothing broken, nothing –'

Then, 'Oh, bother!' she said, fumbling in her apron pocket. 'I've dropped the key to the gate. Oh, bother, bother, bother!'

Mr Nutmouse shone his torch around, nervously scouring the carpet. Eventually, Mrs Nutmouse saw it glinting behind the leg of the chest of drawers. 'There it is!' she said, squirrelling it into her apron pocket.

'Now, hurry, dear! Do hurry!' Mr Nutmouse said, tugging her by the paw.

But as he did so, the mice were bathed in a brilliant pool of light. The bathroom door had opened, and looming above them was a tall, thin figure, wrapped in a white towel.

Chapter Five

The mice froze, rooted to the carpet in terror. Aunt Ivy froze too. She hated all animals, unless they had been turned into coats or gloves or suitcases. But it was mice that she hated most of all. They made her pulse race, and her stomach turn, and her skin crawl, and her eyes pop. And now there were two of them, confronting her, face to face, on the landing. And they were wearing clothes!

Aunt Ivy looked at them in horror, praying that her eyes were deceiving her. One had an apron on, and the other was dressed in a tweed suit, with brown shoes – *shoes!* – and a pair of spectacles strung round its neck. *They're mad mice!* she thought wildly, her brain spinning with fear, then she tightened her grip on the pumice stone in her left hand, raised her arm, and hurled it down upon the Nutmouses as hard as she could.

As the grey missile was released, the mice finally came back to their senses, and they scuttled like they had never scuttled before – over the landing, down the stairs, across the kitchen, and under the dresser, where Mr Nutmouse fumbled with the padlock, his paws shaking.

When the gates opened, he pushed Mrs

Nutmouse inside to safety, and bolted the lock behind them. They could hear Aunt Ivy rampaging upstairs. 'Walter! Wake up! You've got *mice*! You've got an infestation of *mice* wearing clothes!' She said 'mice' with such loathing that Mrs Nutmouse could feel her heart flutter.

Mr Mildew sounded unsympathetic. 'You've been dreaming – now *please*, Ivy, go to bed!' he said; and she eventually did, for it was very late, after all. But next morning the mouse hunt began . . .

From their breakfast table in Nutmouse Hall, the mice could hear Aunt Ivy crashing about Rose Cottage, upturning beds, and bookshelves, and tallboys, trying to find their hideaway. When she started banging about in the kitchen, they went to spy on her through their front gates.

They saw her put down two mouse traps, one by the garden door, and another next to the vegetable rack. (Aunt Ivy always packed mouse traps when she went to the countryside, and in summer she travelled with fly swatters and wasp traps too.) Both the mouse traps were baited with little chunks of stale cheese. *Really!* Mrs Nutmouse thought indignantly. *She must think we're desperate!*

But Aunt Ivy was not going to wait for them to take the bait – she wanted to find them now. She rummaged in the larder, then in the cupboard under the sink. She looked in every drawer, and in every saucepan, she even looked in the wastepaper basket. Then she approached the dresser.

'Stand back!' Mr Nutmouse ordered, pulling

his wife away from the gate. The dresser rattled wildly on the other side of the wall, as Aunt Ivy turned out the drawers and the cupboards. 'Come out!' they heard her mutter. 'Come out, you little vermin! I'll show you what happens to mice who wear tweed suits!'

The Nutmouses trembled. If she moved the dresser away from the wall, she would discover the door to the broom cupboard, and she would discover Nutmouse Hall!

'Oh, Tumtum!' Mrs Nutmouse said weakly. 'What are we to do?'

Mr Nutmouse squeezed her paw very tightly, then the rattling stopped, and there was a sudden glare of light. Aunt Ivy was on her knees, flashing a torch under the dresser. She was so close they could feel her warm breath blowing round their legs – it smelt of coffee.

The torch beam shone back and forth, then rested on the gates. (They were rather fancy gates, similar to the sort one sees in London parks, but of course on a much smaller scale.) The beam lingered there awhile, then a red fingernail reached out and poked the bars.

The mice jumped back into the shadows, sweating with fear. Mr Nutmouse thought of the tiny iron plaque on the gatepost saying 'Nutmouse Hall', and wondered if Aunt Ivy's eyes would be strong enough to read it.

At that moment, Mr Mildew came into the kitchen.

'Walter, what's this?' Aunt Ivy asked crossly.

'Come and have a look!'

Mr Mildew approached her, and she handed him the torch. 'Under here!' she said, getting up to make way for him. 'What's that metal grille down there?'

Sighing, Mr Mildew got down on his knees, and peered under the dresser. He shone the torch about for a moment, then stood up again.

'I've no idea,' he said, sounding preoccupied. 'A ventilation hole, I suppose. Or maybe it's something to do with the sewage. I think there used to be a lavatory down here once, before I moved in.'

'*Eugh!*' Aunt Ivy said, shuddering. They heard her go to the sink, and wash her hands. 'We'll have to get Pest Persecutors to take up the floorboards, like they're doing at my house,' she said.

'I am *NOT* having my floorboards taken up just because you think you've seen a mouse wearing clothes,' Mr Mildew replied, sounding quite unusually emphatic. 'This house is chaotic enough as it is.' Aunt Ivy huffed, and stomped off to the other side of the room to dig about in the ironing pile.

As they heard her retreat, the Nutmouses felt quite weak with relief. 'Come on, Nutmeg, we're safe for now,' Mr Nutmouse said, and led her back indoors to Nutmouse Hall. Mrs Nutmouse made a fresh pot of tea, and they needed several cups each to calm their nerves.

The morning had started off much better for Arthur and Lucy, for they of course had woken up to find five pounds on their chest of drawers. Arthur thought they should spend it all on sweets, but Lucy thought they should save it, in case their father's money ran out altogether.

'If he doesn't make his crumb-gobbling mouse work soon there'll be nothing left for us to live on at all,' she said gravely. 'I heard him telling Aunt Ivy so. So we should keep the money in case we need it to buy basic things, like bread.' Lucy had read a book in which a very poor family lived off bread for a whole month, and she was fully expecting that the Mildew family might soon have to do the same. She'd even cut a recipe for wholemeal rolls out of an old magazine.

'Of course he'll make the mouse work,' said Arthur, who tried very hard never to lose faith in his father. 'And besides, if he doesn't make it work, then five pounds is hardly going to stop us all from starving. So we should jolly well buy sweets while we can.'

This might have turned into something of a row, but at that moment the children heard a splintering crash coming from the ground floor. They dashed downstairs, wondering what it could be. And when they peered round the sitting room door, they found their aunt dragging the old oak chest away from the wall; a china lamp had fallen off it, and lay smashed to pieces on the floor.

'What are you doing?' Arthur asked.

'Looking for mice,' she said sourly. 'It's more than my poor nerves can stand. I came all the way from Scotland because I've got mice there, only to find that this place is infested with them. And yours are different from the ones in Scotland,' she added accusingly. 'Yours wear clothes!'

'Clothes?' Lucy repeated incredulously.

'Yes, clothes!' Aunt Ivy snapped. 'I've seen two of the blighters so far, parading round in suits and aprons as though they owned the place. But there'll be two less by the time I'm through.'

Lucy looked at her intently, wondering if her aunt were mad after all – she and Arthur had sometimes thought that she might be. 'Mice don't wear clothes, Aunt Ivy,' she said firmly.

Aunt Ivy hated being contradicted, so this

made her feel even snappier. She had had a frustrating morning, and now she wanted to take it out on someone. Looking up, she saw that Lucy was holding a five-pound note.

'Who gave you that?' she asked; her voice had a nasty taunt to it.

'A friend,' Lucy said — and it was true, for Nutmeg was a friend, but she could still feel herself going red. Her aunt was eyeing her coldly.

'Well, you must have very good friends,' she said with a sneer. 'Creeping into the house and giving you five-pound notes! My foot!'

Lucy looked at her aghast. The implication was quite clear. If Aunt Ivy didn't believe they'd been given the money, then she must think they'd stolen it. But that was a dreadful thing to suggest!

And quite unfair!

Lucy was about to turn on her heel and march out of the room, which was what she always did when people were being unreasonable – she'd last done it when one of the girls in her class had said that Mr Mildew looked like a tramp. She found walking away to be much better than getting cross – it left her with the agreeable feeling of having the upper hand.

But Arthur was not so restrained, and Aunt Ivy's accusatory tone was making him feel all hot and tickly.

'It *was* given to us by a friend!' he said furiously, his voice quivering.

'And does this mysterious friend have a name?' his aunt asked spitefully.

'Yes!' Arthur replied, almost shouting. 'Her

name's Nutmeg! And she's a fairy! She's a Fairy of Sorts and she comes and gives us things all the time. And she tidies our clothes and mends the roof, and cleans the sink, and we feed her in Lucy's doll's house, and –'

'Arthur!' Lucy said warningly, and then he stopped. But they both knew he had done something awful. Nutmeg had said the magic would not work if they told anyone else about her, and now, of all the dreadful people in the world, Arthur had told Aunt Ivy!

And she was looking at him very beadily. 'You feed this little friend – I mean, fairy?' she asked eagerly, struggling to sound friendly, which had never come naturally to her. She no longer cared about the five-pound note – this was much more interesting. 'What do you feed it with?'

'Nothing,' Arthur mumbled, deciding that he had given away quite enough secrets as it was. But Aunt Ivy's mind had started to whirr.

Much later, when the children were outdoors, Aunt Ivy sneaked up to the attic to investigate. The ceiling sloped down on both sides, too low for a grown-up to stand up under, so she had to crawl across the room on her knees.

She made straight for the doll's house. Bending down, she peered through its kitchen window and saw the little plate, piled with biscuit crumbs. Then she pressed her nose to the drawing room window, and saw the mouse hairs on the sofa, and she looked in an upstairs window, and saw

more mouse hairs on the bed.

Ha! she thought. *Fairies, indeed! As I thought, those idiotic children have been feeding mice! And the cheeky little vermin must have been cavorting around in the doll's clothes!*

Aunt Ivy knelt there, wondering what to do. As long as there was food lying around, the mice were bound to return, so this was clearly the place to snare them. But if she put down a mouse trap, Lucy might remove it. Something more subtle was called for.

Aunt Ivy sat and gnawed her lips for a moment, and then she had an especially nasty idea. *Poison!* she thought cruelly. *Tonight, when Arthur and Lucy have gone to bed, I'll creep back up here, and lay down mouse poison in the doll's house!*

Now mouse poison is a brutal thing, which can

take a mouse quite unawares. At first, he does not even realise he is eating it, then it starts burning horribly at his insides, and if he has swallowed enough there is little chance of recovery, however good his doctor.

Aunt Ivy knew how vicious it was, which is why she thought it was such a good idea. Feeling very pleased with herself, she hurried downstairs, wrapped herself in a long black coat, and went outdoors. She turned left out of the cottage gate and walked purposefully down the snowbound lane, past the duck pond and the war memorial, until she came to the village shop.

As she entered, Arthur and Lucy were just coming out – after all the upset of the morning, Lucy had agreed that they should spend all the money on sweets. But Aunt Ivy did not appear to notice them; there was a strange glint in her eye.

Behind the counter, the shopkeeper, Mrs Paterson, was slowly replacing the lid on a big glass jar of wine gums.

'Do you stock mouse poison?' Aunt Ivy asked tartly, glaring at her.

Mrs Paterson sighed. She did not approve of mouse poison, but she prided herself on stocking everything. She bent her head and started digging in a deep, wooden drawer beneath the till.

'I don't think we do, Mrs Mildew,' she said. 'I certainly haven't ordered any myself and – oh!'

Mrs Paterson stood up again, holding a small red sachet. 'You're in luck, love. We've one packet left.'

Aunt Ivy paid for it hurriedly, and tucked it into her pocket. Then she walked back to Rose Cottage with a skip in her step.

That evening, she bided her time until ten o'clock, then picked up the torch from the hall table, kicked off her shoes, and crept upstairs to the attic. As she poked her head over the top step, she could hear Arthur and Lucy breathing deeply, fast asleep. She slithered on to the floor, and crawled over to the doll's house.

She shone her torch through its kitchen window, and saw the little plate of crumbs on the table. Then she reached into the pocket of her skirt, and retrieved the crumpled sachet of poison. Tearing off a corner with her teeth, she wriggled her thin hand through the doll's house window, and released a sprinkling of the pale powder on to the plate, mixing it into the crumbs with a long red fingernail.

There'll be two very sick fairies in the morning! she thought nastily, turning off the torch.

Chapter Six

The Nutmouses spent the day in Nutmouse Hall, lying low. Mrs Nutmouse polished the great oak staircase, which took her mind off things a little; and Mr Nutmouse dozed in the library, which took his mind off things too. Then there was game pie for supper, and afterwards Mr Nutmouse read Mrs Nutmouse an article in *The Mouse Times*, about lady mice in London having their fur dyed blonde. It made her laugh so much that she got hiccups.

'Oh, Tumtum!' she said, dabbing her eyes with a handkerchief. 'Oh, I do feel so much better! After all, things could be much worse. Aunt Ivy might have moved the dresser, and that really would have been the end of Nutmouse Hall!'

'Quite so,' Mr Nutmouse agreed. 'She's had a good poke around at our gates, and she obviously didn't realise what they were. Our sign must have been too small for her to read. I doubt she'll look under the dresser again. By tomorrow the whole thing will probably have blown over.'

Feeling much more cheerful, Mrs Nutmouse settled down to some knitting, and Mr Nutmouse decided to read some more of the novel he was in the middle of, which was about pirate mice on the River Thames.

He got up to find his jacket, knowing the book to be in its pocket. But he looked in the library, and the hall, and the gun room, and the bedroom, and the bathroom, and the dressing room, and drawing room, and the banqueting room, and the billiards room, and every other room, and the jacket wasn't there.

That's odd, he thought, trying to remember where he had last had it. Then he struck a paw to his forehead. *Blow!* He'd taken it off last night, while they were having their midnight feast in the doll's house. He would have to go back for it, as it had his wallet in it, and his snuff box. He returned to the kitchen, looking rather sheepish.

'I must go tonight, Nutmeg,' he said. 'If the children find it, they might take things out of the pockets.'

Mrs Nutmouse looked at him anxiously. 'But what if Aunt Ivy's still on the prowl?' she said.

'If I keep in the shadows she won't see me,' Mr Nutmouse replied. 'I'll be there and back in five minutes.'

'*We* will be there and back in five minutes,' Mrs Nutmouse said firmly, for she was not letting her husband out on his own. Mr Nutmouse would have argued, but he saw his wife's expression and knew there was no point.

At eleven o'clock, the mice set out. After the dramatic morning, a peace had descended on Rose

Cottage. The lights were off and nothing was stirring. When they reached the hall they could hear the sound of Aunt Ivy's soft snoring carrying through the sitting room door.

Mr Nutmouse was carrying a strong torch, so as to avoid the mouse traps. As well as the two in the kitchen, they passed one in the hall, and three on the upstairs landing. Mrs Nutmouse looked at them contemptuously; she wanted to attach a rude note to one, but Mr Nutmouse wouldn't let her.

When they got up to the attic the children were deeply asleep. On entering the doll's house, Mr Nutmouse found his jacket where he had left it, hanging on the wooden peg on the back of the kitchen door. He put it on hurriedly, patting the pockets to make sure everything was still in place.

An instinct told him to go straight back to Nutmouse Hall, but Mrs Nutmouse was looking longingly at her mop and pail.

'Oh, Tumtum! Aunt Ivy's fast asleep, so surely there can't be any harm in my doing one or two little chores, now we're here?'

Mr Nutmouse looked uneasy. There was no knowing when Aunt Ivy might wake up. And given her mood this morning, he felt that this was no time for them to be at large. But Mrs Nutmouse was so eager, he hadn't the heart to drag her away.

'Oh, come on, Tumtum!' she said, seeing him hesitate. 'Aunt Ivy never comes up here! Anyway, I won't be long. I'll just mop Lucy's shoes, and dust the bedside tables, and darn a sock or two.' She tightened her apron strings behind her back, and fetched the mop and pail from behind the door. 'You sit down and have a little something to eat,' she said bossily.

Mr Nutmouse weakened. The thought of a little something to eat always mellowed him. He scrutinised the meal left out on the kitchen table of the doll's house. It wasn't the usual old shortbread – tonight the crumbs were brown and creamy, quite different. He sniffed the plate, and his face lit up. 'It's chocolate, dear!' he said delightedly. 'They must have bought it with the money we gave them!'

There were few things Mr Nutmouse loved more in the world than chocolate. But since Mrs Nutmouse worried that it made him fat, she seldom allowed him any. 'Are you sure you won't join me, dear?' he asked, licking his lips greedily.

'No, no, Tumtum,' she said. 'You sit down and eat, and I'll get on with things.' Then she happily scurried off to start scrubbing.

Mr Nutmouse sat down at the doll's house table, where the place had been laid. Then he took his novel out of his jacket pocket, put on his spectacles, and opened it in the middle of chapter seven, where his bookmark was. He didn't know what he was looking forward to more – tasting chocolate again, or finding out what happened when the pirate mice stormed the water rats' barge.

He decided to do both things at once. He laid the book on the table by his place, and started to read . . .

No sooner had the first cannonball struck, than the

pirates surged forth over the side of the rats' battered vessel, their pistols firing wildly . . .

Engrossed, Mr Nutmouse reached a paw towards the plate. Then he raised a great dollop of chocolatey crumbs towards his lips . . .

The rats' captain was below deck, distributing muskets among his officers. 'God be with you, rats,' he said, as they heard a second cannonball tear into the rigging . . .

He swallowed a mouthful of crumbs, then automatically reached out for more.

Captain Rattle crossed himself, and led his men towards the burning deck . . .

Mr Nutmouse raised his paw back to his mouth, and bolted down more of the chocolate, but this time he noticed that it tasted odd. Then, quite suddenly, his paws started to shake, and he saw his book drop to the floor. He was feeling very, very queer.

Chapter Seven

Mr Nutmouse could feel a violent, tearing pain in his stomach, as though he had swallowed a piece of barbed wire. Then his head began to pound, as if a hammer were being knocked back and forth inside his skull. And then he began to choke.

Mrs Nutmouse was on the top of the chest of drawers when she heard the sudden explosion of spluttering and gulping, and it gave her such a start she knocked over her pail of soapy water. She jumped to the floor like a cricket, and hurtled into the doll's house to her husband's side.

Mr Nutmouse's face was purple and blotchy. There was sweat streaming from his brow, and his hands were tearing frantically at his tie. He was shaking, and his breath was coming in painful spasms. Mrs Nutmouse started thumping him on the back, and pressed a glass of water to his lips. 'P-P-Poison, Nutty,' he whispered, pointing towards the fateful plate of chocolate. 'Mouse p–' Then his voice was swallowed by another violent fit of spluttering.

Mrs Nutmouse felt a deep dread stabbing through her. *Mouse poison! It can't be!* she thought wildly, for she knew there was no worse horror.

The coughing finally subsided, and Mr Nutmouse slumped exhausted in his chair. He raised his face weakly towards the children's beds. 'Why would they have done this to us, Nutmeg?' he asked gently. 'Surely we never did them any harm.' Then his eyes became lustreless, and the lids drooped.

Mrs Nutmouse knew she must get him back to Nutmouse Hall at once, before he lost consciousness. She put an arm under his shoulders, and prised him to his feet. 'Come on, Tumtum!' she urged, trying to keep the panic out of her voice. 'We must get you home. You'll feel better once you're tucked up in bed.'

But all the while, Mrs Nutmouse's mind was racing. The nearest mouse doctor, Dr Goodmouse, lived nearly two miles away in the next village. You had to cross a ford and then climb a very steep hill to get there; it was a hard enough journey in fine weather, but even the fittest mouse would be reckless to undertake it in the snow. She would have taken any risk for Tumtum's sake, but if she perished on the journey then he would have no one to look after him at all.

Besides, she knew that when it came to poison there was generally little a doctor could do. It often took several days for poison to work its way through a mouse's body, and there was no medicine that could stop its course. Some mice were violently sick for a whole week, and then went on to recover; but if Tumtum had eaten a lot of it he would have scant chance of survival. Mrs

Nutmouse prayed he had consumed only a small mouthful – but then he did so gobble his food.

Her fear deepening, she guided Mr Nutmouse, inch by inch, across the floor. Then she supported him as they stumbled together down the attic steps. But by the time they came to the main stairs he was so weak that Mrs Nutmouse had to slide him down the skirting wrapped in her apron, and then virtually carry him across the kitchen floor to Nutmouse Hall.

He was too exhausted to climb upstairs to his bedroom, so Mrs Nutmouse made a nest for him in the drawing room, on the chaise longue. He tossed and turned all night, retching into a basin and whimpering in pain. His breathing was hot and laboured, and his complexion was a

purplish green.

Mrs Nutmouse pressed a glass of water to his lips, but he couldn't swallow.

Watching his livid face, she felt a cold tremor going down her spine. She knew then that she wouldn't mind if Tumtum never fully recovered; she wouldn't mind if he was invalided, and if she had to nurse him for the rest of his life. But she knew she couldn't face him dying.

'You're going to be all right, Tumtum,' she kept saying to him, but she didn't feel at all sure.

For the next five days, Mrs Nutmouse barely left her husband's bedside. His condition showed no signs of improving, and any glimmers of hope were short-lived. On Monday afternoon, his temperature suddenly went down, but by midnight it was up again, higher than before. On Tuesday morning he managed to eat a few mouthfuls of dry toast, and to swallow some milk, but then he was terribly sick, and for the next two days he didn't eat anything at all.

For most of the time, he was delirious. One morning he asked Mrs Nutmouse to send a telegram to his mother, who had died before they were married. And the next evening he suddenly sat up and hurled a glass across the room, shouting, 'Out! Out!', as if he imagined someone to have broken in.

Mrs Nutmouse had never seen him like this. Tumtum was usually such a calm, mellow mouse, she found his fits terribly unnerving. The anxiety was taking its toll on her: by the fifth day of Tumtum's illness she had lost nearly half an ounce in weight – almost as much as he had. That evening, she tried to eat some bread and cheese, but her stomach was in knots, and she found she could barely nibble a thing.

As the hours ticked by, Mrs Nutmouse started to brood, clutching her husband's paw. She couldn't stop thinking of the children's betrayal. *How could they have done something so dreadful? What had she and Tumtum done to incur such hatred? All we did was to try and make the attic more comfortable*, she thought mournfully. *Surely they couldn't have objected to that?*

Somehow, Nutmeg suspected that Aunt Ivy must have something to do with it; and yet Aunt Ivy could never have known that she and Tumtum were making use of the doll's house unless the children had told her so – and why would they do that?

Mrs Nutmouse felt quite weak trying to make sense of it all. Since adopting Arthur and Lucy she had felt for the first time that her family was complete, and the thought that they had turned on her made her feel quite broken-hearted. Since Mr Nutmouse had been taken ill, all the excitement and bustle had gone out of her; she was quite a different mouse to what she'd been before.

The night stole away, and still she brooded, feeling too overwrought to sleep. *If only I had some sewing to do*, she thought longingly, for sewing always took her mind off things. But she had left her sewing basket in the doll's house. She looked at her watch – it was after midnight. *Everyone will be fast asleep*, she thought. *I don't suppose there can be any harm in going to get it.*

At once feeling a little better for having a sense of purpose, she fetched the torch from the kitchen, and went to the front gate. The cottage was dark and still, no one was stirring. She crept through the kitchen and into the hall, then cocked an ear at the sitting room door and heard Aunt Ivy snoring. Feeling bolder, she went upstairs.

The moon was shining in the attic window, and Mrs Nutmouse could see the children's heads asleep on their pillows; a part of her longed to get close to them, and to brush their hair again with her broom, and yet for the first time she felt wary.

The room looked dusty and neglected, for it was more than a week since she'd last cleaned. The doll's house had been untouched since she and Mr Nutmouse's last visit, and it had a sad, abandoned feel to it. Mr Nutmouse's book was still on the kitchen floor where he'd dropped it, and her sewing basket was where she always left it, in the cupboard under the stairs.

I must get straight home, she thought, tucking the basket over her arm. *If Tumtum comes to he'll wonder where I am.* She hurried out of the doll's house, carefully closing the front door behind her, then picked her way across the attic floor, over a pile of dirty socks.

And she was about to rush back down the steps, when some instinct made her shine her torch up towards the chest of drawers. And she saw a letter, propped against Lucy's hairbrush. It was addressed to Nutmeg.

Nervous it might be another trap, Mrs Nutmouse climbed up a pair of laddered tights which was tumbling from the top drawer, and went to investigate. She looked anxiously towards the children's beds, then unfolded the letter, spreading it out flat on the chest of drawers. The writing was so big she had to take a step back in order to read it.

Dear Nutmeg,

We have missed you so much, please come back. Arthur is very sorry that he told Aunt Ivy about how you visit us, and how we leave you supper in the doll's house, but he only said it by mistake. And he wouldn't have said it if he thought it would make you vanish.

We wish you could come back and make Aunt Ivy vanish instead.

Love from,

Arthur and Lucy.

Mrs Nutmouse read it once, then she read it again; then she felt so overcome she had to sit down on the handle of Lucy's hairbrush to compose herself. At last, everything fell into place. If poor, impetuous Arthur had told Aunt Ivy that a fairy came and ate crumbs in his doll's house, then she might reasonably have suspected that his fairy was one of the mice she had seen on the landing. And then she must have crept up here at night, with murderous intent.

Mrs Nutmouse felt a great rush of relief as

she realised that the children hadn't betrayed them after all. *Oh, bless them, bless them!* she thought. *I knew that dreadful woman must have been behind it all!* She was anxious to get back to Tumtum but she knew she must leave a reply. There was a red pencil lying on the far side of the chest of drawers. She picked it up and held it with both paws, steadying it against her chest as she scrawled a hurried note on the back of the children's letter:

Dear Arthur and Lucy,

Please do not think I have abandoned you. Now that your aunt knows our secret it is more difficult for me to visit, but I am still thinking of you.

Love,

Nutmeg.

Then Mrs Nutmouse added a very defiant P.S. —

I will make Aunt Ivy vanish. I promise.

And she vowed to herself to keep that promise. *I must get rid of her*, she thought, feeling a sudden thrill of determination. *And I will get rid of her . . . but how?*

She bounced down the attic steps, and ran across the landing, and slid down the banister, her mind whirring. She had magnificent visions of herself chasing a terrified Aunt Ivy down the garden path, snapping at her heels, and driving her away from Rose Cottage, never to return. In her excitement, she quite forgot that Aunt Ivy was several hundred times bigger than she was.

Mrs Nutmouse's mind was still galloping as she crossed the hall, and ran under the kitchen door. It was galloping so much that she didn't notice the light had been turned on. *We'll show her who's boss!* Mrs Nutmouse thought, as she sauntered jauntily across the floor. *Tumtum will get better, and then we'll let her know who owns this place!*

She skirted a patch of grease in front of the cooker, then paused to look down her nose at one of the mouse traps. She was feeling quite extraordinarily buoyant.

But then there was a shattering human scream, and in that instant, Mrs Nutmouse saw the tips of Aunt Ivy's slippers just in front of her nose, standing between her and the dresser.

Mrs Nutmouse stopped dead in her tracks.

She knew Aunt Ivy would do something dreadful, yet she felt unable to move. A dark shadow slowly began to engulf her as Aunt Ivy's arm rose upwards, then there was a rapid blur as a teapot came hurtling through the air towards her.

It smashed to the floor millimetres from Mrs Nutmouse's feet, sending splinters of china ricocheting all around. Senseless with panic, she hurtled right over Aunt Ivy's slippers, and ran straight under the dresser with her sewing basket swinging wildly back and forth on her arm.

Oh, what a fool I am, what a fool! she thought, as she wrenched open the gates. *Now she'll know where we are! She'll be back for us again! She'll pull out the dresser! She'll find Nutmouse Hall!*

No sooner had she turned the key in the

padlock, than there was a fierce shaft of light. Aunt Ivy was on the floor, shining her torch directly on to her. Mrs Nutmouse threw herself back from the gate, out of sight, but it could make little difference now . . . Aunt Ivy knew where they lived.

Chapter Eight

Mrs Nutmouse stood shaking in the broom cupboard as Aunt Ivy pulled and heaved at the dresser. At one point, she made it lurch so far forward that all the plates fell off and smashed on the floor. Mrs Nutmouse saw a splinter of china fly through the gate, and then there was a deep thud as the dresser crashed back against the wall.

Exhausted, Aunt Ivy stood awhile, cursing

under her breath. She had seen where Mrs Nutmouse went, so she was no longer in any doubt that the funny metal grid was some sort of mousehole. She wanted to block it up, so the mice would be imprisoned in their lair, and slowly starve to death, but the dresser was too heavy for her to move.

She pondered awhile, then had an idea which pleased her so much that she said it out loud. 'Gas!' she announced, clapping her hands together with glee. 'I'll pump poisonous gas under the dresser, straight into their filthy little hole! We'll see how they like that!' And just thinking about it made her feel much more cheerful.

On the other side of the door, Mrs Nutmouse listened in terror. 'Gas! Gas!' she said to herself, quaking. She imagined clouds of foul, blue poison being pumped through the gates, and curling in under the front door, and advancing through Nutmouse Hall room by room, slowly choking her and Tumtum to death.

Beside herself, she ran inside and locked the front door behind her, putting the draught excluder in place. Then she raced around each of her thirty-six rooms, upstairs and down, locking all the windows, and drawing all the curtains. She found a roll of masking tape in the butler's pantry, and darted back to the hall, using it to seal around the frame of the front door.

But she knew it was hopeless – the gas would find its own way in. It would advance through the joins in the window frames; it would creep in through the pipes and belch from the taps; it would diffuse down the chimneys.

We must escape! she thought. But Tumtum was much too ill to be moved – the upheaval would kill him, even if the gas didn't.

Numb with dread, she went back to her husband's bedside. He was sleeping, and his face looked pale and sallow. All night long the distraught Mrs Nutmouse sat beside him, wondering what to do.

If only Tumtum were himself, she felt sure he would be able to think of something. But his mind was still wandering, and when he opened his eyes he appeared not to recognise her. *Oh what is to become of us?* Mrs Nutmouse thought hopelessly. *Tumtum's delirious and Aunt Ivy might strike at any time!* She put her head in her paws, and closed her eyes tight, trying to shut out the horror. Their chances of survival seemed horribly slim.

But the truth is that Aunt Ivy had no idea what sort of gas to use, nor where to buy it. The only deadly gas she knew about was cyanide, and she imagined it might be hard to come by. Like Mrs Nutmouse, she spent a restless night dwelling on her difficulties; and she was still dwelling on them next morning, when she locked herself in the bathroom.

Aunt Ivy always locked herself in the bathroom for at least an hour, both in the morning and in the evening, usually at just the time everyone else wanted to use it. And she sprayed so many foul-smelling scents and deodorants on herself, that whoever went in afterwards had to press a flannel over their nose.

This morning she was applying something particularly revolting, a hairspray with a sweet citrusy aroma, a bit like compost. It came out in dense green clouds and it made her hair very dark and greasy, just as she liked it. When she had applied several layers, she looked at herself approvingly in the mirror, then made to throw the empty canister into the bin. But something on the label caught her eye.

'DANGER!' it said, in big red letters. 'TOXIC! INHALATION MAY CAUSE SEVERE INJURY!'

Aunt Ivy started to feel a delicious tingle in her spine. *Why!* she thought. *If this gas could injure a*

fully grown human, then it shouldn't be too hard to kill a couple of mice with it! I'll buy some more, and gas them to death tonight!

Then she got dressed much more quickly than usual and went down the lane to the village shop. When she arrived, Mrs Paterson was behind the counter, eating a thick piece of toast; there was butter dribbling down her apron.

'Did the mouse poison do the job, Mrs Mildew?' she asked good-naturedly.

Aunt Ivy did not appear to hear. 'Do you have any more of these?' she asked briskly, slamming the empty hairspray down beside the till. 'I bought it here last week.' As Aunt Ivy leaned towards her, Mrs Paterson picked up a foul, toxic smell, almost like a gas leak. It made her feel quite queasy.

'Sorry,' she said, wrinkling her nose. 'I've none in stock. Next delivery comes at noon on Saturday.'

Aunt Ivy leaned forward on the counter, and looked at her piercingly. 'Reserve me two canisters,' she demanded icily – but then, as Mrs Paterson wrote down the order, Aunt Ivy started to wonder whether two canisters would be enough. There might be more mice than the ones she'd seen – they might have brothers and sisters, and aunts and uncles . . . they might have bred! 'On second thoughts, make that five,' she said grimly. Then she stomped back outside, knocking over a pile of flan cases.

Chapter Nine

Mrs Nutmouse waited all that day, braced for a gas attack, but none came. And yet she felt sure that Aunt Ivy would strike soon.

All the while, the promise she had made to the children rang round and round in her head. 'I will get rid of Aunt Ivy. I will. I will. I *will*.' And now she knew that she must – if she could only think how.

By tea time (which had become a meaningless

time, since Mr Nutmouse was too weak to eat, and Mrs Nutmouse too nervous), she could bear it no longer. If she didn't do something soon, she felt she would go mad.

'Oh, Tumtum! We can't just sit here, waiting to be gassed by that dreadful woman,' she said, anxiously rearranging his blankets. He was sleeping, and much too ill to follow what she was saying, but talking out loud made her feel better all the same. 'We must get rid of her. Oh, I wish I knew how!'

As Mrs Nutmouse was musing, Mr Nutmouse slowly raised one eyelid, then another, then he turned his hollow face towards her. His eyes were sunken deep in their sockets. 'Fetch General Marchmouse,' he whispered hoarsely, his lips barely moving; then his eyelids at once drooped shut again.

'General Marchmouse!' Mrs Nutmouse exclaimed delightedly, clutching her husband's paw as he slipped back out of consciousness. 'Oh, why didn't I think of him before? Oh, Tumtum, you are so clever!'

It was the first sense he had made all week, and Mrs Nutmouse wondered if he'd been talking in his sleep; but it was an ingenious idea all the same, because just repeating the General's name made her feel a warm glow about her. He was considered to be one of the great military geniuses of the age, and in the past he had delivered the village mice from all manner of threats. He once saw off a rabble of looting rats from the granary, even though they out-numbered his mouse soldiers by three to one. After that *The Mouse Times* described him as 'undefeatable', and that was the general view.

He had retired from the army a few months ago, and was by no means in the first flush of youth, but every mouse still had great faith in him. *I suppose he's never gone to war with a human before*, Mrs Nutmouse thought, feeling a flicker of apprehension. 'But anyway,' she said to herself firmly. 'If anyone can save us, then General Marchmouse can.' She decided to go and consult him immediately, while Mr Nutmouse was sleeping. She kissed him on the nose, then ran to the kitchen and flung on her cape.

The General and his wife lived in a disused

gun cupboard in the Manor House, which was owned by an elderly human couple called Mr and Mrs Stirrup. The Manor House was just beyond Rose Cottage, on the edge of the village. Mrs Nutmouse knew the route well, for she and Mr Nutmouse had often dined with the Marchmouses in happier times. Even allowing for the snow she reckoned she could be there and back within an hour.

But as she went to let herself out of the front gates, she heard voices carrying from the kitchen. It was Aunt Ivy and Mr Mildew, discussing *them*.

'I saw one of them with my own eyes, Walter, disappearing under *there*.' Peering out through the gate, Mrs Nutmouse could just see the tip of Aunt Ivy's finger, pointing towards the dresser. 'They've got a nest somewhere behind that metal grille.'

'Hmmm, that's possible,' Mr Mildew said, sounding preoccupied. The only mouse he was interested in was the battery-operated crumb-gobbler he was inventing. The department store which had once sold his grape-peelers wanted to stock it, so if he could only get it working it might make him rich again. But he'd been battling with the digestive system for weeks now, and the mouse was still sicking everything up. It was all giving Mr Mildew the most dreadful headache.

'Can't you help me move the dresser, Walter, so I can get a closer look?' Ivy whined.

Mrs Nutmouse stood behind the broom cupboard door, holding her breath.

'No, Ivy,' Mr Mildew replied firmly. 'That dresser weighs a ton. It hasn't been moved for years, and I'm not going to break my back just because you think you've seen a couple of mice wearing aprons.'

'They weren't *both* wearing aprons – one was in a tweed suit,' she retorted crossly. 'Anyway, I'll be getting rid of them on Saturday.'

'Will you?' Mr Mildew said vaguely.

'Yes,' she replied mysteriously. 'Saturday at noon. When my gas supplies arrive!'

'Oh, *really*, Ivy,' Mr Mildew said, picking up his cup of coffee and making for the door. 'I've never heard such nonsense.'

'I'm going to wipe them out with a toxic hairspray!' she called after him, as he went upstairs. 'One whiff of that and they'll choke instantly!' Mr Mildew was no longer listening, but Mrs Nutmouse had heard every word.

Saturday at noon! she thought, her pulse racing. *That's the day after tomorrow!* She let herself out of the gates, then bolted across the kitchen floor while Aunt Ivy's back was turned. She was feeling quite reckless with urgency.

Mrs Nutmouse hurtled under the door, into the garden. It was a beautiful afternoon, there was no wind, and the snow was shining pink in the twilight. She ran along the edge of the lawn, under the cover of the hedge, and then crossed into the Manor House garden. She took her usual route, through the apple orchard, into the vegetable

patch, over the potato beds, under the lean-to of wintering sweet peas, and then up the clematis on the side of the house, and indoors through the broken windowpane in the downstairs cloakroom.

From the sill, she dropped down on to the lavatory seat, and then to the floor. She crept to the door, and poked her nose out into the long, tiled corridor. It had just been bleached, and the fumes made her eyes water. The door to the kitchen opposite was ajar and she could see the two Manor House labradors curled up asleep together in their basket. When General Marchmouse had first moved in the dogs had been notoriously ill-mannered, and had growled and snapped at his dinner guests. But the General had bashed them both on the nose with his rifle, and now they were said to be more docile.

Even so, the sight of them made Mrs Nutmouse uneasy. So she tiptoed past the kitchen door and then ran down the corridor as fast as she could, skidding and scuttling on the polished tiles, until finally she came to the gun room, which was the last door on the right.

The gun cupboard was a handsome oak chest, nearly two metres tall. There were no guns in it now, as Mr Stirrup had given up shooting when his eyesight started to fail; so the Marchmouses had the whole cupboard to themselves. *Thank goodness, they're at home!* Mrs Nutmouse thought, seeing the light from inside glinting out of the keyhole. She crept round to the back of the cupboard where the Marchmouses had carved out their front door.

It was the General who opened it, wearing a blue and white striped apron. He was holding a rolling pin, and looked flustered. His face was red, and his whiskers were covered with flour.

'Mrs Nutmouse!' he said delightedly. 'Come in, come in! What a nice surprise!' He drew her into the hall; there were spears and shields hanging on the wall, and above the fire there was a glass cabinet containing a stuffed cockroach which the General had shot himself. He propelled her through to the kitchen, where his wife was whisking eggs; she looked flustered too. 'We're expecting eleven of my brother officers for dinner,' the General explained importantly, 'and I'm in command of the fish pie.'

He sat Mrs Nutmouse down at the kitchen

table, and started debriefing her as to his recipe. 'Salmon, cod, king prawns, nutmeg, mature cheddar, a sprinkling of salt and pepper . . .' On he boasted, hardly seeming to notice Mrs Nutmouse's distraught expression.

But Mrs Marchmouse saw it at once. 'Hush, darling,' she urged her husband. 'Mrs Nutmouse has something to tell us.'

The General finally drew breath, and Mrs Nutmouse was able to let the whole dreadful story tumble out. Tripping over her words in haste, she told them how Tumtum was lying at home delirious, poisoned; and about the dastardly Aunt Ivy, and how she was plotting a gas attack at noon on Saturday. And she told them of her fears that in Tumtum's present condition even the slightest

whiff of one of Aunt Ivy's grotesque hairsprays might kill him.

Listening to the drama, Mrs Marchmouse's eyes glazed with horror, while the General's eyes began to blaze. *An adventure!* he thought, feeling his heart stir. The General was a mouse who lived for adventures. They were his lifeblood, his first love, and since retiring from the army he had found them surprisingly hard to come by. *What luck!* he thought, as Mrs Nutmouse finished her terrifying tale. *A war zone just next door, in Rose Cottage!* In his mind, he could already hear the thud of the cannonballs, and smell the gunpowder.

'Oh, General Marchmouse – do . . . do you think you could help us?' Mrs Nutmouse asked nervously.

'Oh, yes, Mrs Nutmouse!' the General boomed. 'I shall assemble an army to repel her. We shall fight from the beams, we shall fight from the rafters! We shall hurl hand grenades from teacups, we shall fire from Wellington boots! We shall never surrender!' Then he thumped his rolling pin down on the table with a mighty crash.

Mrs Nutmouse felt very reassured. He sounded like a mouse who meant business.

Chapter Ten

The General had never taken on a human before and, for all his high spirits, he knew he had quite a fight on his hands. Now that he was retired he kept little ammunition about him, and he would be hard-pressed to get hold of any more at such short notice.

And even if he could, he suspected it would be of little use. The Royal Mouse Army's guns would be much too small to wound a human; a whole round of machine gun fire would barely even scratch an adult's skin.

If he were to launch a sustained attack on the Rose Cottage sitting room, with bombs and hand grenades and cannons, he could probably send the enemy's bed up in smoke. But then the whole cottage might burn down, and Nutmouse Hall with it.

That would not do at all, the General thought sensibly, scratching his forehead with a floury paw. *This will require a much more subtle strategy*. He decided to consult his eleven brother officers when they arrived for dinner. They were all army veterans, like himself, and between them they would be sure to come up with something.

'You are in safe hands, Mrs Nutmouse,' he said reassuringly. 'My colleagues and I have fought mightier enemies than this one.' He could not actually think of any, but nonetheless. 'Now you run along home to your husband, and we will all discuss the crisis over dinner,' he said, patting her shoulder. 'And after pudding, and port, we will proceed to Nutmouse Hall, and set up our military headquarters in the library. Leave your front gates unlocked, so we can come straight in.

'And you, Poppet,' he said, turning to his wife. 'You will accompany us to the Hall, and assist Mrs Nutmouse with the catering. We will bring as much food as we can muster – we must be prepared for a siege.

'Is that clear, ladies?' he asked, when he had

outlined the plan.

'Oh, yes,' they chorused, for the General always spoke clearly.

'Good,' he said. 'Now, synchronise watches. It is just gone twenty-eight minutes before seventeen hundred hours. Mrs Nutmouse, you can expect us to arrive with you at twenty-one hundred hours precisely.'

In actual fact, by the time General Marchmouse and his party trooped through the gates of Nutmouse Hall, it was nearly ten o'clock. (Dinner had been later than expected, as the General had forgotten to turn the oven on.) Each mouse was dressed in his red and green military uniform, and carrying a big canvas kit bag and an assortment of ammunition.

General Marchmouse was the most generously armed. He had a pistol in a holster on his belt, and a long string of grenades looped round his chest. Another officer, a peppery grey mouse called Colonel Acorn, was carrying a sword in a silver scabbard encrusted with little red jewels. Mrs Marchmouse was bringing up the rear, trundling a smart shopping trolley which her husband had made for her out of one of Mr Stirrup's matchboxes. He'd painted the box blue, and for the wheels he'd used two big yellow buttons borrowed from Mrs Stirrup's sewing basket.

The trolley was full of provisions – there was bread, butter, milk and eggs, the remains of the fish pie, a cold leg of lamb, a tin of shortbread, two dozen freshly baked scones, and a chocolate cake with crystallised cherries on it. There were also some tins of peaches and pineapples, and a box of strawberry creams.

'Did you have any trouble getting across the kitchen?' Mrs Nutmouse enquired, taking their coats in the hall.

'No trouble at all,' the General said breezily. 'The enemy is lying low.' Mrs Nutmouse felt a pang of unease at hearing him sound so jaunty; she knew Aunt Ivy wouldn't lie low for long.

Mrs Marchmouse disappeared to the kitchen, while Mrs Nutmouse led the men to the library. They swiftly took the place over. General Marchmouse hung a sign saying 'War Room' on the door, and then the officers started rearranging the furniture.

The sofas and chairs were all pushed back against the wall, and Mr Nutmouse's desk was pulled into the middle of the room, and covered with toy soldiers. Then the General and his officers started shuffling the soldiers back and forth, and helping themselves to Mr Nutmouse's cigars.

They were enjoying themselves immensely. It was just like old times, when they had all been in barracks together. But as Mrs Nutmouse bustled in and out of the library bearing trays of cake and cocoa, she felt more and more agitated. The night was stealing away, and Tumtum was tossing feverishly on his chaise longue, his health still in grave danger; but the officers in whom she had placed such faith were behaving as though they were on holiday.

'General Marchmouse, what is your plan of attack?' she asked, as she cleared away a third round of refreshments.

The General looked slightly put out at this question, because the truth is he had no plan at all. Fighting stoats and rats was one thing, but a human enemy required a wholly different strategy. And though he and his brother officers had racked their brains all through dinner, they hadn't come up with one.

As a result, the General felt as though he was on the defensive, and it was a position he disliked. 'I am not at liberty to divulge tactics, Mrs Nutmouse,' he said pompously, puffing his chest.

'Oh, of course, I quite understand, General,' Mrs Nutmouse replied tactfully, taking away his empty mug. 'Well, anyway, I'll be in the drawing room, tending to Mr Nutmouse, if you need me.' General Marchmouse huffed dismissively, but his brow was furrowed. Mrs Nutmouse was only a housewife, of course, but it occurred to him that perhaps he should have consulted her. After all, she knew more about Aunt Ivy than he did.

'One minute, please, Mrs Nutmouse,' he called after her, as she made for the door. 'You may be able to assist us, after all.'

The General swept a pile of maps off the sofa, and Mrs Nutmouse sat down, balancing her tray on her lap. 'We are building up a profile of the enemy, Mrs Nutmouse,' he said, standing over her. He was speaking very slowly, for he imagined that Mrs Nutmouse might find this sort of talk hard to understand.

'We are drawing up a list of her weak points,' he continued. 'The things that might frighten her, the areas in which she might be most vulnerable to attack. I just wondered, Mrs Nutmouse, if you happened to know of some?' The General looked down at Mrs Nutmouse eagerly, for he hadn't been able to think of any himself.

Mrs Nutmouse thought very hard. Weak points? Somehow she had never thought of Aunt Ivy as weak. She wasn't physically weak, at any rate – you could tell from the way she had shaken the dresser about.

And what might frighten her? Mrs Nutmouse thought. *What would frighten any fully grown human? An elephant, perhaps? . . . A lion? . . . A hurricane?* She pursed her lips in concentration; it was very difficult. But then the answer suddenly dawned on her.

Of course! she thought, remembering the one thing that Aunt Ivy was very frightened of indeed. In fact, it was something she knew her to be absolutely terrified of – a terror which had been quite clear on that fateful night when Aunt Ivy had seen herself and Tumtum on the landing.

But Mrs Nutmouse was worried that the General might think her silly for suggesting it.

'Does anything spring to mind, Mrs Nutmouse?' he asked impatiently, fingering his whiskers.

'Well, yes, there is one thing, General,' she said, blushing. 'She's . . . Well, it may sound strange, but –'

'Come on, now, Mrs Nutmouse,' the General urged her. 'Time is precious!'

'Well, General,' Mrs Nutmouse said falteringly. 'The truth is . . . the truth is, Aunt Ivy is *terrified* of mice!'

The other officers all looked up in astonishment. '*Mice*, Mrs Nutmouse?' General Marchmouse repeated, incredulous. 'The enemy is afraid of *mice*? Afraid of *us*?'

'Quite so, General,' Mrs Nutmouse replied. 'You should have seen the commotion when she caught sight of me and Tumtum on the upstairs landing. The way she carried on, shrieking and wailing, and waking the whole household. Why, you'd have thought she was more frightened of us than we were of her!'

'Were either you or your husband armed at the time, Mrs Nutmouse?' the General asked. 'Were you carrying guns, or what have you?'

'*Armed?*' Mrs Nutmouse repeated, astonished. 'Of course not, General! What an extraordinary suggestion!'

'So why was she frightened of you?' the General asked, looking very confused.

'She just happens to be frightened of mice, General,' Mrs Nutmouse replied. 'Some humans are, I'm told, even fully grown ones. I suppose it might explain why they invented mouse traps.'

'Hmmm.' General Marchmouse was pensive. This changed everything. Forget the grenades and the pistols – they could frighten the enemy simply by saying 'Boo!' But frightening her was one thing. Driving her away from Rose Cottage, running in terror of her life, might be harder.

General Marchmouse's brain was pounding. He was undefeatable, *The Mouse Times* had said as much, so he must think of something. Failure was not an option. Forgetting all about Mrs Nutmouse, he walked over to the desk, and gathered the other officers round him. They bent their heads together, and started debating earnestly, using all sorts of military mumbo jumbo which Mrs Nutmouse couldn't understand.

But as she sat watching them from the sofa, clutching her tea tray, a dazzling idea began to play itself out in her mind's eye, and it became more dazzling by the second.

'General Marchmouse,' she cried, 'I –'

'Just a moment please, Mrs Nutmouse,' the General said airily. 'We are trying to formulate a plan.'

'Well perhaps you would like to hear *my* plan,' Mrs Nutmouse replied.

They all turned to face her. 'Well, fire away, then,' the General said grudgingly, vowing to himself that this was the last time he'd let a woman into his War Room. He drummed his paw impatiently on the table while Mrs Nutmouse began.

'Given that Aunt Ivy is afraid of mice, General, I wonder how many mice it would take to make her leave the cottage for good? I mean, she saw Tumtum and I, and now she's determined to kill us. And if she saw all twelve of you, she would probably try to kill you too. But suppose she were to see dozens and dozens of mice, hundreds of them, flying at her out of every nook and cranny, running all over her, digging into her hair, and her clothes, going up her skirt, and under her shirt, and down her sleeves, and under her collar, and climbing up her necklace, and somersaulting from her bracelets, and swinging from her earrings . . . Well – don't you think *that* might make her flee?'

The officers stared at her admiringly, and even the General had to acknowledge that it was a first-class idea.

'A capital plan!' he said joyfully. 'We will overwhelm the enemy with numbers! We will conscript every mouse in the village who is young and fit enough to fight, and we will charge as one!' The General banged his stick on the table, feeling very pleased with himself. This might go down in the history books as his cleverest battle plan yet!

But then he caught sight of Mrs Nutmouse, and suddenly remembered that, strictly speaking, it had all been her idea. 'I had been about to propose just such a strategy myself, Mrs Nutmouse,' he said chivalrously. 'Thank you for prompting me.'

Chapter Eleven

Arthur and Lucy had spent the day in a state of great anticipation, wondering when Nutmeg would carry out her promise to make Aunt Ivy vanish. They had no idea what methods Fairies of Sorts used to get rid of aunts, but they suspected that Aunt Ivy's disappearance might prove rather dramatic.

'Do you think she'll try and frighten her

away?' Arthur asked Lucy when they woke up to find Nutmeg's note on the chest of drawers.

'I shouldn't think so,' his sister replied. 'Nutmeg must be much too small to frighten her. If she's going to make her vanish she'll have to do it by magic. She'll probably just wave a wand and make her disappear in a puff of smoke.'

'Where would she make her go?' Arthur asked.

'Oh, I don't know,' Lucy said, trying to sound more laid-back about it than she felt. 'If she's feeling merciful she might just magic her back home to Scotland — but perhaps there's an especially horrid place where fairies magic away all the people they don't like.'

Arthur shivered: it was a terrifying thought. The children spent the day loitering round downstairs, monitoring Aunt Ivy round the clock lest they miss the moment of her vanishing. They even trailed after her when she went to the village shop, but they made sure never to get too close, as they expected she might go up in smoke at any minute and they were frightened of getting singed. And yet by supper time she was still there. She spent the evening sitting at the kitchen table, filing her nails and ranting about how she was going to exterminate Rose Cottage's rodents by squirting citrus-flavoured hairspray under the dresser.

By the time the children climbed up the attic stairs to go to bed they were beginning to feel quite despondent. Nutmeg had had a whole day to make Aunt Ivy vanish, so why hadn't she done it? 'You do think she *can* do it, don't you?' Arthur asked tentatively; but by now even Lucy was starting to have doubts.

It was up to the officers to carry out Nutmeg's promise, and once she had provided them with a basic plan of attack they sat up late into the night thrashing out tactics. Shortly after midnight, the General and Colonel Acorn went to make a reconnaissance of the ground floor of the cottage, which they now referred to as 'the battle zone'. They sketched out detailed plans of the kitchen and the hall, then they crept into the sitting room while Aunt Ivy was sleeping and noted down the exact position of each bit of furniture, even the log basket. When they got back to Nutmouse Hall they pinned their maps up in the library and the General spent the next hour or so sticking red pins in them.

Mrs Marchmouse scuttled in and out with trays of cocoa, while Mrs Nutmouse sat with Mr Nutmouse as he tossed and turned on his sick bed in the drawing room, with no inkling of what was going on.

It was not until the small hours of the morning that a final strategy was formed. General Marchmouse stood before his officers, a bacon sandwich in hand, and ran through it point by point. It was a complicated plan, so each mouse took notes in a special Royal Mouse Army code.

At dawn, seven of the officers, led by Colonel Acorn, would leave Rose Cottage and spend the morning enlisting recruits (200, or thereabouts) from the village. General Marchmouse and the

remaining four officers would mount guard at Nutmouse Hall, in case Aunt Ivy made any premature advances. (The plan did not specify what they would do if she did.)

The new recruits would be marched back to Nutmouse Hall by one o'clock and be divided into eleven platoons, with each platoon under the command of an officer. Then, at some point during the afternoon, whenever the coast became clear, the army would march into the Rose Cottage sitting room and take up position.

One platoon would spread out behind the books in the bookshelf, one would lie in wait beneath the armchair, one would crawl through the tear in the sofa cover, and hide in the stuffing. Another would lurk in the chimney, and another in the log basket; there would be platoons in every corner of the room, poised to attack. The General would mount guard behind the flowerpot on the mantelpiece, from where he would have a sweeping view of the battlefield.

And thus would the mice bide their time until evening, when Aunt Ivy finally retired to the sitting room, and started getting ready for bed. Then the General would fire his pistol, signalling the charge, and they would all race towards her in one squealing, scrabbling, fearless stampede.

The General could not make any plans beyond that, as he did not know how Aunt Ivy would react. So he adopted a policy of hoping for the best.

'When she sees the size of our army she will run for her life,' he said confidently.

'It's a capital strategy, General!' Colonel Acorn said, raising a mug of cocoa to him. 'Quite astoundingly brilliant, even by your standards!'

'Hmmm. I suppose you could argue that it's one of my more imaginative ones,' agreed the General, who had by now quite forgotten that the idea owed anything at all to Mrs Nutmouse.

And yet one of the officers, a Brigadier with tousled ginger hair and smart leather boots that rose up to his knees, seemed uneasy. 'One thing concerns me, General,' he said. 'When the enemy gets into bed, she might put her light out straight away. Then she wouldn't be able to see us, and if you were standing on the mantelpiece, you wouldn't be able to see the platoons. We'd be fighting blind.'

The General looked pensive, it was keen thinking. 'Have you anything to suggest, Brigadier?'

'Well,' the Brigadier said, 'I suppose we could all carry candles, but they might be something of a fire hazard when the time came to charge.'

'Much too dangerous,' the General agreed. 'We don't want to burn the cottage down.'

'Why don't we dress the troops in fluorescent uniforms?' Colonel Acorn suggested.

'It's a good idea, Colonel,' the General said. 'But how are we going to get hold of 200 fluorescent uniforms by tomorrow night?'

The officers considered this problem for a moment, and none could solve it. But then the General remembered the child's bicycle he had seen propped outside Rose Cottage, by the garden door, and he pursed his lips. At that moment, he heard Mrs Nutmouse and Mrs Marchmouse passing outside in the corridor. 'Ladies! A moment please!' he bellowed, calling them into the library.

'Mrs Nutmouse, do either of the Mildew children possess a cycling jacket?' he asked mysteriously. 'You know, the garish sort that humans wear when they cycle on the roads at night.'

'Why, yes, General, Arthur has one,' she said. 'A fluorescent orange one, hanging on the back of the kitchen door.'

'And would he miss it if we were to borrow it on a permanent basis?' the General asked.

'I shouldn't think so,' Mrs Nutmouse said, trying to imagine what this was all about. 'He never uses his bicycle because it has punctures in both tyres.'

'Good!' the General said. Then he turned to Mrs Nutmouse and Mrs Marchmouse, looking very grave. 'I need your help,' he said. 'If we were to retrieve that jacket, could you turn it into 200 mouse-sized uniforms by thirteen hundred hours tomorrow afternoon?'

'Goodness!' Mrs Nutmouse said, and Mrs Marchmouse shook her head. Two hundred uniforms by lunch time tomorrow! It was out of the question.

Mrs Marchmouse looked at her husband regretfully. 'I'm sorry, darling, but even if we worked non-stop, we could probably only manage five uniforms by then. Sewing trousers and jackets isn't as easy as it looks, you know. There's the legs and the sleeves, and the hems and the cuffs and the –'

'Yes, yes, I understand all that, Poppet,' the General interrupted, even though he didn't really understand at all. 'But what about something less ambitious? Armbands, let us say! Could you make 200 fluorescent armbands by tomorrow afternoon?'

'Oh, yes!' Mrs Marchmouse said eagerly. 'We could run up 200 armbands in no time, couldn't we, Mrs Nutmouse?'

'Of course,' Mrs Nutmouse agreed. 'They wouldn't even need hemming.'

'Excellent,' the General cried, rubbing his hands together. Then he turned back to face the officers. 'Very well, gentlemen! From now on, we shall refer to this operation as the Charge of the

Bright Brigade, after that glorious human battle that took place in, er, in . . .' The General looked around, hoping someone might prompt him, but everyone looked blank. 'Er, well,' he said hurriedly, 'in the days of Queen Victoria!'

The officers supposed the General was thinking of the Charge of the Light Brigade, which happened not to have been very glorious at all. But no one liked to contradict him, so they all accepted his version of events.

'The Charge of the Bright Brigade!' Colonel Acorn cried, raising his sword in the air. And then all the other mice cried it too; except for Mrs Nutmouse, who had already dashed off to find her sewing basket.

* * *

The cycling jacket had been left on a coat peg, high up on the kitchen door, but the officers managed to reach it by climbing up the strings of an apron which had been hung beside it. Then they teased it off the peg, and dragged it back under the dresser. Colonel Acorn used his sword to cut it into little pieces, small enough to fit through the Nutmouses' front gates, then they carried all the fragments into the drawing room of Nutmouse Hall, where Mrs Nutmouse and Mrs Marchmouse set to with their scissors.

The lady mice worked without pause, sitting by Mr Nutmouse's bedside. How Mrs Nutmouse longed to shake Tumtum awake, and tell him that General Marchmouse was going to rouse a whole army to save him, but he was much too weak to

take such excitements on board.

Some of the officers managed to grab a few hours sleep during what remained of the night, stretched out on soft leather chairs in the library, but at the first hint of dawn the hustle and bustle began. Colonel Acorn and his party set off for the village to round up the troops, and the other officers waited tensely for their return, pacing back and forth in the War Room.

As the minutes ticked by, the atmosphere in Nutmouse Hall thickened. By the time the drawing room clock struck one, Mrs Marchmouse and Mrs Nutmouse had made 220 armbands (they ran up a few extra ones for good measure); but Colonel Acorn had not come back. And by the time the clock struck two, General Marchmouse had shuffled his toy soldiers back and forth so many times that his eyes were beginning to boggle; and still there was no sign of the troops.

Finally, at ten past three, the officers heard a loud commotion outside. The General straightened his beret, and marched out of the front door towards the gates. And through them he saw a great rabble of recruits, their cold noses glinting softly in the gloom beneath the dresser. He tried to count them, but couldn't. There were scores, hundreds of them, a multitude of excited, jabbering rodents.

The General peered eagerly into the crowd, picking out faces. There was the baker, armed with a rolling pin! There was the fireman, carrying his hose! There were the school mice, brandishing water pistols! And there was the police mouse, with his truncheon! The whole village had turned out on Mr and Mrs Nutmouse's behalf.

It's an army! the General thought ecstatically. *It's an infestation! And* I, *the undefeatable General Marchmouse, am in sole command!*

'Hello, there, General,' Colonel Acorn cried, pressing his nose through the gate. 'Quite a crowd we whipped up this morning, 203 at last count. Sorry we couldn't get back earlier, but that Mildew fellow was loitering about in the kitchen, burning toast by the smell of it, and we had to wait ages before it was safe to march everyone across.'

'Good work, Colonel,' the General replied, brusquely pulling open the gates. The officers came through first, then the village mice surged after them, chattering raucously. They were herded into

Nutmouse Hall, then straight through to the ballroom where they were divided into platoons and each allocated an armband. Finally, General Marchmouse climbed up on top of Mr Nutmouse's concert piano, to make a rallying speech.

'Quiet, please!' he bellowed, stretching back his shoulders, *'QUIET PLEASE!'* The General did not like shouting; before he retired, he had always had a sergeant to do it for him. He filled his lungs with air, and tried once more. *'QUI-ART PLEASE!'* Eventually, the clamour subsided, and the mice turned to face him, all agog as to what was in store for them.

The General cleared his throat solemnly. He always addressed his men before a battle, he felt it good for morale, and he was especially pleased

with the speech he was about to make now. He had been rehearsing it secretly in the billiards room.

'Mice,' he began slowly. 'You are gathered here today to face an enemy greater than any of us has ever faced, and crueller than any of us has ever known. But the purpose of our expedition is not to injure, nor to maim. It is simply to be *seen*. The enemy is deadly, but her weakness is fear. Fear of *us*.

'And if she sees enough of us, leaping out from the bookcase, springing from the window sill, descending from the chimney, spilling out of the stuffing in the sofa, deluging her from every corner of her boudoir . . .'

The General paused for effect. He needed to make his strategy sound more foolproof than it was. '. . . Well, then she is *bound* to retreat!'

One of the mice, standing towards the back of the crowd, raised a grubby paw. 'Is that why we're wearing these armbands, General? So we can be seen?'

'That is correct, young man,' the General replied. 'We shall be charging the enemy by night, and her den may be ill-lit. The armbands will ensure that every one of us makes an impression. Be he large, or be he small, every mouse among us *must* be seen.'

The General hesitated again; he was sure he had planned a much longer speech than this, but he had suddenly lost his thread. Flustered, he started to improvise.

'Mice! You have come here as volunteers, to defeat an enemy, and avenge the poisoning of a friend. As you march into battle, think upon what has befallen our beloved Mr Nutmouse, lying wretched and immobile on his chaise longue.

'And think upon the consequences if Aunt Ivy remains untamed. At noon tomorrow, her gas supply will arrive, and what hope for Mr Nutmouse then? But remember, above all, that this is not merely a battle of mice against man. It is a battle of right versus wrong; it is a battle of courage versus cowardice . . .'

General Marchmouse had become very red in the face, and was starting to wheeze. He drew his sword from his scabbard, and flourished it wildly in the air. 'It is *The Charge of the Bright Brigade*!'

A deep volt of electricity surged through the army. Punching the air with their bright orange sleeves, the soldiers chorused back the war cry: 'The Charge of the Bright Brigade!' And there was not a mouse among them who was not longing for it to begin.

Chapter Twelve

There followed a tense few hours, as the mice waited for an opportunity to march unseen into the Rose Cottage sitting room. Colonel Acorn and the Brigadier mounted guard at the gates of Nutmouse Hall, monitoring the constant comings and goings on the other side of the wall.

All afternoon, Aunt Ivy sat at the kitchen table, filing her nails and drinking a foul smelling herbal tea. The children appeared at five o'clock to make some toast, and took it away without a plate; and after that Mr Mildew came and scavenged in the fridge, then retreated back upstairs with a bowl of cornflakes.

'Fascinating, isn't it?' Colonel Acorn said, peering through the bars. 'These human creatures don't seem to sit down to meals like we do. They graze, like cows.' (Colonel Acorn and his wife lived behind the flour bins in the village shop, so he seldom saw humans in their domestic habitat.)

'Yes, most odd,' agreed the Brigadier. 'But mine aren't at all like that.' The Brigadier lived in the airing cupboard of a grand house on the other side of the village, and he was rather proud of *his* humans. They had dinner in a dining room, by candlelight, and they had a maid to wait on them. 'I believe that some humans are more civilised than others,' he concluded thoughtfully.

The Colonel agreed this was probably true. And then they both held their noses as Aunt Ivy started smoking a menthol cigarette.

Back in Nutmouse Hall, the ranks were beginning to feel restless. They had been buoyed up by General Marchmouse's speech, but two hours later and they were still cooped up in the ballroom. Mrs Marchmouse was scurrying among them, dispensing tots of sherry, and as the alcohol warmed their blood they felt more boisterous than ever.

'When can we be off, General?' was the constant cry, and the General wished he could answer. But there was nothing to do but wait. He checked his watch constantly. Five o'clock . . . six o'clock . . . seven o'clock, and still no go ahead from the officers at the gate.

Eventually, shortly before nine, Colonel Acorn reappeared. 'All clear, General,' he reported excitedly. 'Aunt Ivy is in the bath; Mr Mildew is in his study; and the children have gone to bed.'

The General turned to face the troops. 'Arise!' he roared magnificently. 'The time has come to show the enemy what we're made of!' The mice at once scrabbled to their feet, and were briskly marched outside. Mrs Nutmouse and Mrs Marchmouse stood in the hall, watching them go. A lieutenant brought up the rear, and slammed the door shut behind them. Then Nutmouse Hall suddenly felt very quiet and still.

A green felt cap lay on the flagstones in the hall, dropped by one of the school mice, but otherwise the army had left no trace of itself. Mrs Nutmouse felt a sudden foreboding. *Oh, please bring them all home safely*, she prayed silently. Then, feeling a sharp chill, she went to replace the draught excluder by the front door.

The kitchen light was off when the mice spilled out of Nutmouse Hall's front gates, but the moon was shining through the window and it made their armbands glow. With the General leading, the army crossed the floor in a tight crocodile, making a detour around a pool of spilled tomato ketchup, and then crept into the hall. The General put a paw

behind his ear; he could hear Aunt Ivy splashing about upstairs in the bath.

She had left the sitting room door open, and a reading lamp in the corner was casting long shadows across the floor. The room was cluttered, with lots of places to hide.

The sofa on which Aunt Ivy slept was on the far side of the room, in front of the window, and at either end of it there were coffee tables strewn with books and magazines. There were armchairs on either side of the fire, and beside one of them was a log basket full of old newspapers. On the opposite wall was the bookcase, so over-laden that the shelves were beginning to sag in the middle; and heaped in front of it were all Aunt Ivy's suitcases — one had a long green stocking snaking out of it.

Seeing the battlefield lying before them, the mice all felt a little awed. Every one of them knew, by instinct, that the thing to do when you saw a human was to run. But tonight they would be charging straight towards one, into hands that could squeeze them to pulp, and towards feet that could kick them so hard that they would go twirling and swirling into the air, until they smacked against a wall. Even the bravest among them felt his stomach flutter.

The General's stomach was fluttering too, but no one would have guessed it. 'Officers, take up your positions!' he barked. Then he flicked his stick under his arm, clipped his heels together, and marched them forward.

Each officer knew where his platoon was to

hide, and within five minutes they had all clambered into position. There were mice everywhere, even inside Aunt Ivy's sponge bag, but they were so carefully hidden that there was not a mouse to be seen.

Keeping very still, they settled down to wait. It was a tense time for everyone, particularly for Colonel Acorn's platoon which had crawled through the tear in the lining on one of the sofa arms. They were hiding in the stuffing which was thick and coarse; it got up their trousers and under their collars, itching mercilessly.

Things were more comfortable for General Marchmouse, who had hoisted himself up a picture-ladder on to the mantelpiece, where he was hidden behind a dusty pot plant.

From there, he had watched the platoons take up their positions through his field glasses; and then, in the deep hush that followed, his sleepless night started to catch up with him, and his eyelids got heavier and heavier.

I must refresh myself before the battle, he thought, beginning to stagger slightly on his feet. He hated being tired, but since retiring he'd become increasingly prone to it. He drew his sword, and, reaching up, cut off one of the soft, green leaves fanning above his head. Then he lay down on it to rest. 'Just a quick nap,' he said to himself drowsily, and within a few seconds he was fast asleep.

All round the room the eleven platoons crouched

stiffly, waiting for the first scent of the enemy, and for the crack of General Marchmouse's pistol signalling them to charge.

Eventually, after nearly an hour, they heard the *thud, thud, thud* of human feet on the stairs. They twitched their noses nervously, and picked up a sickly smell of bathroom lotions, then Aunt Ivy entered the room. The door made a loud creak as she pushed it behind her, but not loud enough to wake the General who was in a deep, deep sleep, dreaming of all the glorious battles he'd won in his youth.

The other 214 pairs of eyes all peeked out of their hideaways, wakeful and riveted. Aunt Ivy was dressed in dark green pyjamas with a red dressing gown tied tightly at the waist, and she had on a thin gold bracelet and a necklace of fake pearls, each the size of a mouse's head, and a silver lizard hanging decoratively from each ear. (Aunt Ivy always wore a lot of jewellery, even in bed.) The army felt uneasy, she wasn't like the other humans in the village. There was something strange about her, almost reptilian.

Aunt Ivy walked towards the window, and tugged the curtains tighter together. The platoon on the sill cowered back into the shadows, as one of her pink fingernails poked through the gap.

Then she walked towards the bookcase and started digging about in one of her suitcases. There was a platoon of mice hiding in the bottom of it, and one of them felt her finger brushing the back of his jacket. Eventually, she found what she was looking for, a tortoiseshell hand mirror and a pair of metal tweezers. She kicked off her slippers and lay back on the sofa, then started plucking the little grey hairs from her chin.

Aunt Ivy did this once a fortnight, and it was very tedious and fiddly. As she held the mirror up to her face she screwed up her eyes, and stuck out her tongue, and stretched her legs right out, pressing her feet against the arm of the sofa. Her toes pushed Colonel Acorn's platoon deeper into the stuffing, squashing the mice so tight that they could hardly breathe.

Why the devil doesn't the General give the signal to charge? the Colonel wondered despairingly.

At that moment, Aunt Ivy's big toe wriggled its way right through the hole in the lining, and he saw a gnarled toenail heading straight towards him. The Colonel squirmed, frantically trying to get out of its path, but he was trapped in the stuffing, barely able to move. The toe advanced on him like a tank.

He watched it loom nearer and nearer, dizzy with dread. And then, just as it was about to squash him, he opened his mouth and sank his teeth into Aunt Ivy's skin. Chomp! He got her just below the toenail, and bit in so deep he had to wrestle his jaw free with his paws.

For a split second, nothing happened, and the Colonel wondered if he hadn't dreamed the whole thing. But then there was a sudden shriek. 'Fleas!' Aunt Ivy cursed, rubbing her toe, but she was about to face something much more alarming than

that. For her cry had woken the General, who was scrambling to his feet, frantically fumbling for his field glasses.

Standing beside the flowerpot, he quickly took stock of the battlefield. He saw the Brigadier, peeking out from behind a botanic encyclopaedia on the bookshelf; he saw the glint of a sword in the log basket; and the soft glow of twelve fluorescent mice crouching up the chimney.

With adrenaline coursing from his head to his tail, the General rushed forward to the edge of the mantelpiece, and fired his pistol in the air. The battle had commenced.

Chapter Thirteen

Nursing her toe on the sofa, Aunt Ivy did not hear the General's pistol going off, as the gun was smaller than her fingernail. But the mice heard it loud and clear, and as the explosion echoed round the room they sprang from their hiding places shouting, 'Charge!', and ran madly towards her.

She sat mesmerised, her eyes darting left and right, as the full might of General Marchmouse's army appeared before her, out of thin air. First, she saw little orange lights on the bookshelf, then a dozen fluorescent mice flew from the shelves. She saw mice bursting from the window sill, and the waste paper bin, and the log basket. She saw them spilling out of the chimney, and springing from her suitcases, and pouring out from beneath the armchair, like a flood.

This is just a dream, a horrible dream, she thought, desperately trying to calm herself. *Any second now, I am going to wake up. Come on, Ivy! Wake up! Wake up!* But she didn't wake up, and the mice kept coming.

Then she felt something ticklish on her legs. She looked down to see the Colonel's dishevelled platoon, clambering out of the stuffing, and

scurrying up her shins. Finally, Aunt Ivy screamed. And she screamed, and she screamed, and she screamed; and she batted her arms and kicked her legs, but to no avail. For now there were mice running all over her.

They scuttled up the sleeves of her dressing gown, and down the collar of her silk pyjamas. They burrowed underneath the towel on her head, tickling her scalp with their claws, they hung from her bracelets, they somersaulted like acrobats on her necklace.

Staggering to her feet, she caught a glimpse of herself in the mirror above the fireplace – there were mice perched on her shoulders, there were mice nuzzling her ears, there was even a mouse clambering on to her forehead. And there, standing boldly on the mantelpiece, was a mouse carrying a gun! *This* must *be a dream*, Aunt Ivy thought again. *It must! It must!*

Suddenly, there was the sound of footsteps in the hall. General Marchmouse pointed his pistol in the air, and fired it three times, signalling the retreat. His bullets hit the ceiling, but they were too tiny even to graze the paint. The army scampered back to their hiding places so fast that by the time Mr Mildew poked his head round the door a few seconds later, there was not a mouse in sight.

'Ivy! What on earth's going on?' he demanded. 'Anyone would think you were being murdered!'

'I am, Walter! I am!' she shrieked, looking

down her body in horror. 'I am being murdered by *mice*!'

'Mice? What mice? Really, Ivy, are you feeling quite all right?'

'They were here, Walter,' she cried. 'They were! They were! There were dozens, hundreds, thousands of them! A whole army of fluorescent mice. And they were *armed*, Walter, they were carrying guns!'

'Ivy,' Mr Mildew said gently, standing in front of the bookcase, inches from the Brigadier's nose. 'It is late, and you are overtired. Try and get some sleep, and then if you're still feeling out of sorts in the morning we'll go to the doctor and get something to calm your nerves.'

But Aunt Ivy was not listening to him.

'It's your wretched children,' she stammered, '. . . leaving crumbs in the doll's house, encouraging them . . . giving them ideas . . . breeding an infestation . . .'

'Now go to bed, Ivy,' Mr Mildew said firmly, then he shut the door and went back upstairs. He supposed his poor sister-in-law was having some sort of a turn, but he had spent another frustrating day trying to make his Hungry House Mouse work so he was feeling less sympathetic than he might otherwise have been.

The General waited tensely behind the flowerpot, and when he heard Mr Mildew's study door bang shut he stepped forward and let off his pistol again to signal the second charge.

All at once, the mice leapt back out of their hideaways and raced towards Aunt Ivy. They knew now that she was more frightened of them than they were of her, which made them even bolder. The Brigadier climbed up on to her nose, and the Colonel sat on her chin.

When she shrieked, he could see right inside her mouth. *Goodness!* he thought, looking at her huge tonsils, and the deep black chute beyond. *If I were to fall down there I might never get out again! I might have to live the rest of my life inside Aunt Ivy's stomach!* He shuddered, and jumped down on to her shoulder.

Blind with terror, Aunt Ivy ran to the kitchen and fled through the garden door. 'Walter! Walter! Do Something!' she shouted, as she stumbled across the lawn, her feet sinking into the snow. Then she tripped over and collapsed under a pear tree, with 215 fluorescent mice scuttling all over her.

Fearing Mr Mildew might reappear, General Marchmouse stood on Aunt Ivy's forehead and fired his pistol three times again, ordering a second retreat. As the mice were hurtling back into the kitchen, a light flashed on in the attic. Arthur and Lucy appeared at the window, and peered down at their aunt in amazement.

Then Mr Mildew's head poked out of the window on the upstairs landing. 'Ivy, what the deuce is going on now?'

'Mice, Walter!' she wailed miserably. 'It's those confounded orange mice again!'

'There *ARE NO MICE*,' Mr Mildew said,

speaking very slowly and firmly, but not altogether unkindly. 'Now come back inside. Please, Ivy. For all our sakes.'

The chill night air bit into Aunt Ivy's skin, and slowly brought her back to her senses. It was a still, cloudless night, with no breeze. She looked down at her dressing gown, at her arms, at her hands. There were no mice there; only a few of their little hairs which her eyes were not sharp enough to see. *Perhaps I did imagine it all*, she thought weakly. *Perhaps Walter's right, perhaps I am going mad.*

'Now come inside,' Mr Mildew called down again. Finally, Aunt Ivy got up, and limped back towards the cottage. She hesitated a moment at the garden door, her hand trembling on the knob. 'Pull yourself together, Ivy,' she said to herself, firmly.

'There is no such thing as a fluorescent mouse. Walter was right, you are overwrought.'

Taking a deep breath, she walked into the kitchen. And from all round the room, she was watched by hundreds of twinkling eyes. General Marchmouse had repositioned his army.

As Aunt Ivy pulled the door shut behind her, she heard a rustling sound coming from the laundry basket. She swung round, and saw something orange glinting through the wicker.

The General, who was standing on the oven, fired his pistol, and the mice made their third assault, each platoon springing from a different hideaway. They came at her from the sink, from the vegetable rack, from the waste paper basket and from the teapot on the dresser – one platoon even sprang out of a Wellington boot.

But this charge was much briefer than the others, for Aunt Ivy seemed so frightened that the General felt it unsporting to carry on very long, and he withdrew his forces after less than a minute.

The army evaporated, but Aunt Ivy remained huddled on the doormat awhile, too fearful to move. Then she walked across the room on tiptoes and gingerly picked up the telephone. The mice watched from their hiding places as she rustled through the telephone directory, then hurriedly dialled a number.

'Is that Mr Glengle's Round-the-Clock Cabs? . . . Good . . . I need a car at once . . . Twenty minutes? No, I need one now! I'll be dead in twenty minutes . . . Where to? Home, damn it. To

Scotland. And send me the fastest driver you've got.' Then there was a sharp click as she replaced the receiver.

Chapter Fourteen

Aunt Ivy thought better of waking Mr Mildew again; instead she hastily scribbled him a note on the back of an unpaid gas bill and left it on the kitchen table. Then the mice crept after her into the sitting room, and watched from behind the door as she hurled her clothes into her suitcases, and dragged them into the hall. When she heard the taxi spluttering to a halt outside, she tossed her black overcoat on over her dressing gown, and went out of the door wearing slippers.

The mice all scrambled up the curtains on to the window sill and pressed their noses to the glass, watching avidly. The taxi had its headlights on full beam, and a tall, thick-set driver in a tweed cap got out. Aunt Ivy walked up the path towards him and pointed back towards the cottage, gesturing him to collect the luggage. They heard him come inside, then saw him return to his car carrying three suitcases. Then he came back for the other two, flung them all into the boot, and opened the passenger door for Aunt Ivy to get in.

The driver got inside and started the engine, then there was a belch of exhaust fumes, and Aunt Ivy was gone. The mice watched as the headlights

faded into the night, and they knew the battle was won. 'She's gone!' they cried, waving their orange armbands in the air, and jumping up and down with glee. The Colonel was so elated that he made to kiss the General, but then he stopped himself, and they both looked a little embarrassed.

The army trooped back to Nutmouse Hall, singing triumphantly, but the General lingered behind a moment in the sitting room, surveying the battlefield. Besides some dust which had fallen from the chimney, there was nothing to show that any unrest had taken place. No fallen bodies, no bloodied barricades; the General wished all his battles could have been like this one.

He would not let it be forgotten in a hurry. *I must telephone through to* The Mouse Times *first thing in the morning, and make sure it carries a full report*, he thought loftily, beginning to compose what he would say. He decided he would leave out the detail about his falling asleep on the mantelpiece.

Back in Nutmouse Hall, Mrs Nutmouse and Mrs Marchmouse had been waiting on tenterhooks by Mr Nutmouse's bedside, wondering what was happening in Rose Cottage. They had heard the General's pistol going off, and they had heard Aunt Ivy's terrible shrieking, and they had prayed all the while that the army was winning. It had certainly sounded that way.

It was long after midnight when they heard the first of the troops returning through the front gates. Then the drawing room door burst open, and the General strode in. 'The night is ours, ladies!' he cried delightedly. 'Aunt Ivy has been soundly defeated; she's retreated to Scotland in a taxi!'

Mrs Marchmouse flung herself on him, weeping with joy. 'Oh, darling, you are so clever and brave! And to think that I imagined I might never see you again!' The General smiled broadly, but then he looked down on Mr Nutmouse, lying palely on the chaise longue, and his expression turned to one of concern.

'How is the patient, Mrs Nutmouse?' he asked gravely.

'His temperature is a little down, General, and he's stopped being sick,' she said. 'There is definitely *some* improvement. I do hope he wakes up soon – his spirits are bound to improve when he hears that Aunt Ivy has gone.'

Even as she said it, Mr Nutmouse's head moved stiffly on the pillow. Very slowly and tentatively, he opened his eyes, then he blinked rapidly, like a creature who has lived all winter underground and burst up through the earth's surface on the first day of spring.

'Did I hear you say Aunt Ivy had gone, dear?' he murmured, turning to his wife. He looked anxiously at the clock. 'Oh, deary me. Have I been asleep long? I feel quite ravenous. I hope I haven't missed tea.'

Mrs Nutmouse gazed adoringly at him, hardly daring to believe her eyes. He was still very pallid, but the sweat had lifted from his brow, and his eyes were clear and bright, quite unlike yesterday.

'Oh, Tumtum!' she cried joyfully, kissing him on his nose, which was healthy and moist again. 'Yes, Aunt Ivy has gone! And you have missed more than tea! You've missed a week of teas, and a week of dinners, and a week of breakfasts and lunches and elevenses, and you've got so little tummy left that I'll have to think of another name for you!'

Mr Nutmouse looked quite astonished. He patted his stomach, and wondered where it had gone. He could remember going up to the attic the other night, and tucking into a plate of chocolate which had tasted rather queer, but since then everything was just a blur.

'What's all that commotion?' he asked, hearing the mice clattering about in the hall.

'That's the soldiers, Tumtum!' Mrs Nutmouse

said. 'You've slept through a battle!'

'Goodness!' Mr Nutmouse said, feeling more bewildered by the minute. Then his stomach started rumbling violently, and Mrs Nutmouse joyfully raced off to find him something to eat. *The poor troops will be starving too!* she thought busily. *What on earth can I feed them all?*

But when she entered her kitchen, she found the problem had been solved for her. A pork sausage, a full six inches long, had been discovered abandoned in the Mildew's grill, and the Colonel and the Brigadier had carried it back to Nutmouse Hall on their shoulders. There was also a whole slice of bread, which had needed four mice to carry it, and a knob of butter the size of a golf ball.

Mrs Nutmouse instructed the officers to lay

out the feast in the banqueting hall. The room had last been used on her wedding day, and this morning her mood was so celebratory that she wanted to see its shutters thrown open again. 'Left out of the ballroom, Colonel, then third door on your right – it's the room with the chandelier and the family portraits,' she explained, and then she scurried off to the kitchen to find some mustard.

Two barrels of cider were retrieved from Mr Nutmouse's cellar, and then the feast got underway. The Colonel carved the sausage with his sword, and the Brigadier sliced the bread with a cutlass, and there were enough hotdogs for each mouse to eat until his stomach was fit to burst.

Mrs Nutmouse took a slice of sausage through to Mr Nutmouse in the drawing room,

and he wolfed it all down, with a strong cup of tea. The General sat with them, giving them a blow by blow account of the battle.

'Quite ingenious, General, quite ingenious,' Mr Nutmouse kept muttering with his mouth full. And Mrs Nutmouse and Mrs Marchmouse laughed until they wept when the General recounted how the mice had swung from Aunt Ivy's earrings, and turned somersaults on her pearl necklace. 'Oh, poor woman!' Mrs Nutmouse cried, dabbing tears from her eyes. 'Poor, poor woman!' But when she remembered the horror through which she'd put Tumtum, it was hard to feel very sorry for her.

Finally, when the General felt he had been congratulated enough, he made to take his leave. 'We'd best be getting home, Poppet,' he said, turning to his wife. 'It will be dawn before we know it.'

'Goodness, yes,' she replied, remembering that she hadn't slept for – how long was it? One day, two days? She was too tired to remember, and she suddenly longed for her warm bed in the gun cupboard. 'We'll need a hot water bottle,' she thought, thinking that all the fires would have long since died out.

'I'll go and dismiss the mice,' the General said, getting to his feet. And yet he found himself oddly reluctant to go. Much as he loved Mrs Marchmouse, the adventurer in him dreaded returning to his quiet life at home.

'Is there anything else I can do for you, Mr Nutmouse?' he asked hopefully.

'Oh, no, General, I think you've done quite enough,' Mr Nutmouse replied.

But Mrs Nutmouse was blushing. 'There is something, General,' she said hesitantly. 'But I'm afraid it might be asking rather a lot of you – I'm sure you're yearning to get home.'

'Not if duty calls, Mrs Nutmouse,' he replied stiffly.

'Well,' she went on. 'It's just that Mr Nutmouse and I have been trying so hard to keep Rose Cottage in order – to mend the radiators, and seal the cracks in the windowpanes, and patch the leaks in the ceiling, and dust and scrub and all that, so that the children can live decently. But it's all proven too much for us. I'm sure you noticed what a pitiful state the place is in. But with a whole army of you here, and all so healthy and strong, I thought, perhaps . . . Well, perhaps *you* could have a go at getting the place shipshape.'

The General beamed, delighted to be given another chance to take command. 'Leave it to me, Mrs Nutmouse,' he said. 'Give us an hour or so, and we'll have Rose Cottage looking fit for a mouse! My army numbers a plumber, and an electrician, and a carpenter, and a window glazer, and an engineer, and a thatcher, and a plasterer —'

'But would they be able to tackle human-sized things?' Mrs Nutmouse asked doubtfully.

'Of course they would,' the General replied. 'I called the electrician round to the Manor House just last week, to fix the overhead light in the gun room. He broke into the fuse box and sorted it out in no time; he said it was only a tripped switch. And when a pipe started leaking on to our gun cupboard, the plumber climbed up and patched it for me with some of his wife's old copper saucepans. If humans had any sense they'd always employ mice for the fiddly jobs like that.'

'Quite so!' Mr Nutmouse agreed. 'We could put every human labourer out of business!'

'Hmmm! No wonder they're so wary of us then,' the General said, making for the door. Then he marched off to the ballroom to start bossing everyone around.

From Nutmouse Hall, the Nutmouses and Mrs Marchmouse could hear the distant hum of activity, as the army advanced through Rose

Cottage, putting things to rights. At one point, there was a loud hiccup, followed by a deep whirring noise. 'Sounds like they've got the old boiler working again!' Mr Nutmouse said admiringly. Then there was a great crashing and rattling in the kitchen, as dozens of mice scrambled about scouring the cooker.

They went through each room, mending and scrubbing; and when they found the tin mouse in Mr Mildew's study they took it to pieces and gave it a whole new digestive system so that it could keep down all the crumbs it gobbled. They tested it on Mr Mildew's desk, which was always covered with crumbs, and it worked very efficiently. *I must get one for the gun cupboard*, the General thought. *Much better than a vacuum cleaner.*

Last of all, they carried out a lightning attack on the attic. The plumber unblocked the sink, the engineer repaired the engine on Arthur's train set, and the carpenter sawed little pieces off one of the shelves in the wardrobe, and used them to board one of the broken windowpanes where Mr Nutmouse's repairs had come undone. The Colonel had discovered half a sack of coal in the woodshed, and the army carried enough lumps upstairs to light the attic fire.

Just as the flames were beginning to flicker, two great human fists emerged from Arthur's bed, and stretched slowly into the air. With a start, the General realised that dawn had crept up on them; the sun was pouring through the window.

'Downstairs, quick!' he ordered, and all at

239

once the army started hurtling towards the attic steps. The General brought up the rear; and had Arthur sat up and opened his eyes a moment sooner, he would have seen an elderly mouse charging across his bedroom floor brandishing a pistol.

Chapter Fifteen

It was the most wonderful day in Rose Cottage. When Arthur and Lucy woke up they discovered that Nutmeg had been back with a vengeance, lighting fires and mending trains; and then they went downstairs and found the whole cottage transformed. But the best surprise of all came when they opened the sitting room door and realised that Nutmeg had carried out her promise after all: Aunt Ivy had vanished.

'Do you think she's gone for good?' Arthur asked, hardly daring to believe it.

'It looks like it,' Lucy said joyfully; for all their aunt had left behind was a pair of tweezers. (She had also left a lizard earring which had fallen off during the fray, but the General had taken it back to hang in the gun cupboard as a souvenir.) 'Nutmeg said she'd do it, and she jolly well has.' As the reality sank in, they both fell silent for a moment; they hadn't realised Nutmeg was quite so influential.

'I wonder what she did to make her so frightened,' Arthur said, for they'd both heard Aunt Ivy shrieking in the night. 'You don't think she *really* sent hundreds of fluorescent mice to attack her, do you?'

'Of course not,' Lucy said firmly, for that was too terrible a thought. Even Aunt Ivy didn't deserve that. And yet Nutmeg moved in such mysterious ways that secretly Lucy wouldn't have put anything past her. But somehow neither of the children felt it right to question Nutmeg's methods; they just felt very happy she had come back.

Presently, Mr Mildew appeared. 'Good morning,' he said cheerfully; he was holding his tin mouse, and looking immensely pleased with himself. He'd expected to spend another day struggling in vain to get it going, but when he'd turned it on after he woke up it was gobbling beautifully, and keeping everything down. He couldn't for the life of him remember how he'd done it – but now he was going to rush out to the

post office to have it couriered to the manager of the department store in London. *I might be rich again*, he thought – and the idea made him feel just a little bit giddy.

'There was some sort of racket last night wasn't there?' he asked, pulling a pair of Wellington boots on over his pyjamas and trying to remember what it was all about.

'It was Aunt Ivy,' Lucy said. 'She ran into the garden, screaming that she was being attacked by orange mice. I should think everyone in the village must have heard her. And now she's gone.'

'Gone?' Mr Mildew repeated disbelievingly. He looked in the sitting room, then in the hall, then in the kitchen, and sure enough Aunt Ivy wasn't there. Then Lucy spotted the note she'd left on the table, weighted under the milk jug. The writing was scrawled and messy; it had clearly been written in a great hurry. Mr Mildew sat down and fished his glasses from his pocket, then read it out loud.

Dear Walter,

Your cottage is infested with wild mice — hundreds and thousands of them, possibly millions. They are armed and they are orange and they are out to kill. They are living in the bookshelf and the sofa and the sink and the laundry basket — they are everywhere. They have colonised the entire cottage. I am leaving for my own safety — I advise you to do the same.

Ivy

'Poor old Ivy,' Mr Mildew muttered. 'Orange mice, indeed!'

In Nutmouse Hall, the army had returned to the ballroom, where Mr Nutmouse was doing the rounds, thanking each mouse in turn for rescuing him. He was walking cautiously, with a stick, but he was already feeling much stronger.

The mice finally disbanded, crossing the kitchen floor while the Mildews were poring over Aunt Ivy's letter. The General was the last to leave, hovering a while at the Nutmouses' front door. 'I could stay here and stand guard,' he suggested to Mr Nutmouse. 'Just in case — well, in case of any further trouble . . .'

'Oh, no, General,' Mr Nutmouse said kindly,

taking him by the paw. 'You have saved my life and I am not going to let you do anything else for us. But please take this –'

Mr Nutmouse walked stiffly towards the oak chest by the fire, and picked up a long brass telescope. 'It belonged to my great-great-great grandfather,' he said, presenting it ceremoniously to the General. 'He served in the Royal Mouse Navy – he travelled far and wide along the stream, all the way to the next village, I'm told.'

The General was very stirred. 'Thank you, Mr Nutmouse,' he said solemnly. 'I will always treasure it.' Then he closed his eyes and sent up a silent prayer that there might soon be another battle, so he could have occasion to use it. And he prayed the same thing all the way home to the gun

cupboard; but not out loud, for fear of upsetting Mrs Marchmouse.

When the Marchmouses had gone, Mr and Mrs Nutmouse shut their front door and retreated to the kitchen. It was breakfast time, so Mrs Nutmouse boiled a kettle for tea and made some buttered toast, and a big pot of porridge, and two boiled eggs, and a round of pancakes. And as she bustled about, she thought how nice it was that she and Tumtum were alone again.

'He's a queer fellow, that General Marchmouse,' Mr Nutmouse said philosophically, watching her laying everything out on the table. 'Anyone would think he actually enjoyed going to war, and risking life and limb and all that.'

'Well, I suppose some mice crave adventure,' said Mrs Nutmouse. 'But I hope we don't have another one, Tumtum. I don't feel I'm quite cut out for them.'

'Oh, I don't think there'll be any more adventures coming our way, dear,' Mr Nutmouse said confidently. 'We've had more than our share. From now on we'll just live happily ever after.' Mrs Nutmouse agreed with him; and then they sat down to breakfast and put all the trouble from their minds.

The End

EGMONT PRESS: ETHICAL PUBLISHING

Egmont Press is about turning writers into successful authors and children into passionate readers – producing books that enrich and entertain. As a responsible children's publisher, we go even further, considering the world in which our consumers are growing up.

Safety First
Naturally, all of our books meet legal safety requirements. But we go further than this; every book with play value is tested to the highest standards – if it fails, it's back to the drawing-board.

Made Fairly
We are working to ensure that the workers involved in our supply chain – the people that make our books – are treated with fairness and respect.

Responsible Forestry
We are committed to ensuring all our papers come from environmentally and socially responsible forest sources.

**For more information, please visit our website at
www.egmont.co.uk/ethical**